going

going

going
going

NAOMI SHIHAB NYE

Greenwillow Books
An Imprint of HarperCollinsPublishers

Going Going

Copyright © 2005 by Naomi Shihab Nye

Half-title and title page illustrations copyright © 2005 by Esther Pearl Watson
All rights reserved. No part of this book may be used or reproduced in any manner whatsoever without written permission except in the case of brief quotations embodied in critical articles and reviews. Printed in the United States of America. For information address HarperCollins Children's Books, a division of HarperCollins Publishers, 1350 Avenue of the Americas, New York, NY 10019.
www.harperchildrens.com

The text of this book is set in 11-point Adobe Garamond.

Library of Congress Cataloging-in-Publication Data

Nye, Naomi Shihab.
Going going / by Naomi Shihab Nye.
p. cm.
"Greenwillow Books."
Summary: In San Antonio, Texas, sixteen-year-old Florrie leads her friends and a new boyfriend in a campaign which supports small businesses and protests the effects of chain stores.
ISBN 0-688-16185-5 (trade). ISBN 0-06-029366-7 (lib. bdg.)
[1. Political activists—Fiction. 2. Small business—Fiction.
3. San Antonio (Tex.)—Fiction.] I. Title.
PZ7.N976Go 2005 [Fic]—dc22 2004010146

First Edition 10 9 8 7 6 5 4 3 2 1

 Greenwillow Books

In memory of Carl Brenner,
grandson of the founder of Solo Serve,
founder of Alamo Orchard Company.
He always asked, "How is your book going?"

We miss you, friend.

contents

A Prayer

the world is
changing into
what the world
changes into
when the world
changes you
into the world

<small>MARK PETERS</small>

From the mountains to the plains,
all the towns are wrapped in chains. . . .

<small>GREG BROWN</small>

1 ~ justin's italian ice

What if Florrie had not been boycotting TCBY for being a franchise and had stopped there, instead of wandering down to the San Antonio River to cozy, familiar Justin's Italian Ice?

The boy ahead of her in line jingled a handful of quarters. He wore sandals, knee-length beige shorts with many pockets, a thick green T-shirt, and smelled terrific. He was much taller than Florrie, about her age, sixteen, or a little older, and wide at the shoulders. He was staring straight ahead at the list of flavors over the counter, mouthing them perceptibly . . . pistachio, almond nougat, cantaloupe, lemon.

This caused Florrie to watch his succulent mouth very closely. He turned and grinned. "Hey, what's best?"

She felt flustered. "It's all good. Depends on what you like."

"Very helpful."

He turned to face the counter.

"Mexican vanilla!" he said.

"But that's ice cream, not ice," said Florrie. "Which do you want?"

"I don't know. I thought I wanted ice cream. What about you?"

Florrie shivered. "Ice," she said. "Definitely ice." September had been very hot so far. Hotter than August, even. He motioned to her to step ahead of him while he made up his mind.

Florrie said hi to Justin, the boy who worked there. The shop was named for his father, who had opened it years ago, and had the same name. Justin lived a few blocks from Florrie in old downtown San Antonio. They had known each other since they were small. "Hey," she said. "Kiwi in a medium cup, please." Then, "I saw your photograph in that show at the Guadalupe—yours was the best!" She tried to pull a napkin from the container with her free left hand.

The other boy stepped up to the counter and echoed her order—"Kiwi—in a medium cup"—then looked down to count the money in his hand.

Justin raised his eyebrows at Florrie. "Stalker," he mouthed.

She went to sit outside at a small table with iron legs. A cluster of pale-skinned tourists—where were they from, Nebraska? Minnesota?—huddled together by the river looking at a map. Florrie could hear them mention the Alamo and had to control her desire to tell them to go immediately across the little bridge and head right up the stairs.

The boy stepped out the door behind her, stared at the river a moment, then sat down at the table next to Florrie's. He looked at her as he licked his spoon. "I wasn't really going to sit here," he said.

"I was going to take this and leave. But I wanted to ask you something. Are you by any chance the person who was on the ten o'clock news a few nights ago? You look kind of like her. . . . "

Florrie gulped. She was sure he heard it.

"Don't tell me your dad runs Sam's Club," she said.

He laughed. "Hardly! He manages the big Marriott." He paused. "And my mother runs the Gap at North Star Mall." He was grinning, staring at her hard.

Florrie felt momentarily speechless.

Then he said, "Just kidding. My mother teaches eighth-grade English."

"But the Marriott is true?"

"Yup. The Marriott Rivercenter hotel. You know it?"

"I guess so!" Florrie said. "How could I not? It has like one thousand rooms."

He was licking his spoon. "Kiwi's good, by the way."

She said, "Your dad's hotel allows dogs. That's nice of them."

"How do you know that? Did you take a dog there?"

Florrie shrugged, "I ride the elevators sometimes. I've ridden them during dog shows. Sometimes I go to dog and cat shows. Do you ever go? Once I rode an elevator with two Saint Bernards—I almost expected them to press the buttons. It seemed nice that a hotel would let them in."

"Were you visiting someone?"

She paused. It sounded strange. "No. I always go in buildings. Check them out. I enjoy—architectural details. Also I like knowing which conventions are in town, for instance those potato people last week all wearing potato-shaped badges, did you see them? Wandering around is sort of my hobby."

He hadn't looked away, so she continued. "The Gunter and Menger Hotels are my favorites. Plus the Saint Anthony, of course. The old ones. Big chains own them now but they are still the old ones."

"And what did you find at my dad's Marriott, besides dogs?"

Florrie thought he seemed very curious.

"Well, the usual stuff. It's an okay place, but there are too many Marriotts! No offense. There are like four or five downtown right now! I mean, there are too many hotels, period! But once everything gets standardized, it gets less interesting. Don't you think? Fewer kids growing up might feel like they could ever open a hotel of their own, the way Mr. Menger or Mr. Gunter did."

"The truth is," he said, "till I saw you on the news that night, I'd never honestly thought about it. I mean, who wants to open their own hotel? Do you know anybody?"

Florrie did not. But if it were a different world, she might have.

They were both scraping the bottoms of their cups. She wished they'd gotten the large size. She was very glad the Italian ice had been frozen so solidly—it had taken longer to eat it.

What happened next surprised her completely.

She was certain that he was secretly thinking, *You are such a dud*, but instead he asked, "Have you ever heard that the Menger Hotel is haunted?"

"Of course! There's a whole book about it! Thirty-two different documented ghosts supposedly live in there."

He said, "I know, can you believe it? My uncle once saw the lady ghost playing the piano in the lobby."

"Are you serious?" said Florrie. "So did my grandfather! I always walk through the lobby, hoping to see her, and I never do. And wouldn't you like to see that cowboy ghost who appears in the rooms of businessmen staying alone? Do you know about him? He's standing there when the men come out of the shower. He scares them so much they run down to the desk in their boxer shorts! He's supposedly wearing a fringed jacket, staring out the window toward the Alamo, and turns his head to say, 'Are you with us or against us?'"

"No way!"

"I swear!"

He laughed. Florrie thought he had the richest, most musical laugh she'd ever heard.

"I missed that," he said. "But tell me this. Have you tasted the Menger's mango ice cream that they've been making for, like, a hundred and forty years? The stuff that the White House flies in for dinner parties?"

"Of course!" She was impressed that he knew this.

"Well, maybe you'll meet me in the Menger garden someday? They have those tables with umbrellas? Kiwi one day, mango another. My treat. Yes?"

Her head whirled. She scrawled her number and e-address on a napkin.

He grinned. "And you can tell me more about—this thing you're doing."

His name was Ramsey. He lived in Alamo Heights.

2 ~ swoon

After meeting Ramsey, Florrie wandered around downtown through the late-afternoon crowds feeling electrically charged, as if she had stuck herself into a socket but didn't die. Her skin and eyes felt lit up. She didn't feel this way very often. She took deep breaths at the crosswalk. She slapped her own cheek lightly and said, "Calm down, girl."

She wondered if Ramsey had read the recent newspaper story about an albino ghost living in the rodeo barns at the Coliseum. What a great name, *Ramsey, Ramsey*. She turned it over inside her head, tasting it. Didn't she have some faraway Arab cousin named Ramzi?

Florrie dodged down to river level from the street again and crossed a little arching bridge. Where were those cool breezes? They were really taking their time. Huge cypress trees rose gracefully from the water's edge. She patted a gnarled trunk as she passed it. "Hey tree, I met you when I was three, remember?" Florrie had never been shy about talking out loud when she was alone. Now and then people saw her do it, but she didn't care very much. Sometimes it was easier to think that way.

The grassy bleachers at the Arneson River Theater were vacant today. Florrie climbed up to street level at La Villita, the little "old-town" section of downtown, across the street from HemisFair. She still had some extra time before she had to be at work at her mom's restaurant, El Viento. And now she was *far* too pepped up to get there early and do her homework.

Florrie had always wished she could have seen the stucco and stone houses that stood on the HemisFair grounds before the city wrecked them.

A few were still standing, in use as gift shops or restaurants. Some of the elders in Florrie's own neighborhood six blocks away had lived in those houses growing up. To think that a city would just *erase* an entire neighborhood, even to make a world's fair back in 1968, was very upsetting. The fair had only lasted one year.

Years later when the Alamodome was built, a few blocks to the west, the same thing happened again. Ruben Romo, Florrie's father, was so upset about the Alamodome obliterating another neighborhood that he wrote some controversial feature articles for the *San Antonio Express-News*, where he worked. He interviewed people who were being kicked out of their homes. They were given only around twenty thousand dollars in exchange for each house. The city kept saying things like, oh, it's a poor neighborhood, we'll relocate the people, they'll have new lives in a better spot. *But,* Florrie thought, *that was their spot, you know? How rude! Even if houses did need paint, so what? The city could have built the Alamodome somewhere else. Like in a vacant field.*

But Florrie knew that vacant fields weren't really vacant. They had grasses, they had bugs. Whole worlds lived under their skin of soil and pebbles. Still. Almost nobody cared about them.

Near the Tower of the Americas, with its sleek elevator carrying tourists to the observation deck and its rotating restaurant, an artist had recently planted some tiled stone steps in a hillside. It looked as if a house had been buried in a landslide. Only the blue steps were left, poking out at odd angles, surrounded by green grass. *What a great art piece,* Florrie thought. She hadn't seen it before. *But what a sorrow.*

Florrie strode as fast as she could, breathing deeply, skipping over the boulevard divider on Alamo Street. She could feel the blood pumping hotly inside her legs and chest. She closed her eyes to picture Ramsey's face. She couldn't *believe* he had recognized her from the news.

Maybe it was a good thing she had cut her hair.

He might not have recognized her with her old hair. One day before the rally that got covered on TV, Florrie had stared into El Viento's mirror and decided to make a change. Shoulder-length hair was common and messy. You had to be touching and smoothing it a lot, flinging it back over your shoulder. She was always filing it behind one ear. It got dirty from so much touching.

Hair ornaments seemed embarrassing—bows, clips, bouffant fabric puffs for ponytails. You might as well walk around in a tiara or a halo.

So before the supper rush, Florrie had marched into Sandy's Hair Salon around the block from El Viento and asked for "the shortest they could do without shaving. So it stands up straight like a little crop of grass."

Sandy had clucked her tongue and asked, "*Mija*, does Della know?"

Florrie told a roundabout non-lie, "My mother knows I am a girl with my own mind. And she respects that."

But Della Hamza didn't know her daughter would materialize in the restaurant with a brown bag of hair clippings just as the flour tortillas began rolling off the press for dinner—Della froze as if she had been stung by a mighty bee. "*Mija, por que?*" she shouted. "Why have you made yourself look like a police cadet?" Two diners turned their languid, long-haired heads to stare.

Florrie shrugged. "It's what I want. Sorry! I didn't mean to shock you." She offered the sack of hair, grinning.

"Aye-yi-yi. I *hate* it. My pretty girl is gone!" Della started crying. "And how often do you think you'll have to get it cut to keep it looking like that? You'll have to pay ten dollars of your own money every month now, if you want to keep it looking so . . . terrible."

Florrie knew that lots of people paid money for hair maintenance. Two or three of her friends highlighted their hair regularly. That must cost *something*.

"It's okay, Mom," Florrie said, "and now I'll be able to concentrate on the issues."

"Issues?"

"My work. The stuff I like to think about."

Della rolled her eyes. She patted them with a napkin. "Think about *me* next time, not your buildings. Preserving my peace of mind. I do not see what hair has to do with your . . . issues. Makes no sense at all. *Pobrecito,* put on your apron. Isn't this your night to bus?"

True, Florrie's brother, charged out of the back of the restaurant and stopped, stunned, when he saw his sister. His eyes went very wide. "Hey! Are you *joking*? Mom, did she have a sex change? Now you have two sons! Gee! Did you know there is a whole website for people with your haircut?"

Florrie didn't answer him. Their mother tipped her own head to the side to look at Florrie from another angle and said, "Thank God it will grow."

* * *

Florrie was still a little startled to see her own reflection in windows. She moved among the tourists so smoothly she felt as if she were floating a few inches above the pavement. She passed the block where the Post Office Café used to stand. Her grandfather had told her so many stories about that place she could almost see it. He used to eat biscuits at its counter. Her mother had drunk her first cup of coffee there.

Florrie felt the odd flush that she sometimes experienced walking down a city street. All these people—each one with memories and wishes and, if they were lucky, beds and pillows and messy drawers and things they hadn't done yet that they hoped to do. You could feel a swell of unexpected love for *everyone* sometimes, even if they didn't all look like someone you wanted to talk to.

Florrie still had fifteen minutes left, so she headed over to the Nix hospital. She liked the engraved golden elevators inside the cool lobby. They seemed palatial, serene. Sometimes she would step inside the Nix just to visit them. Today the air-conditioning hit her in a bracing wave. She glided into an open elevator as if she had a mission. The person nearest the buttons, a man with a yellow bouquet, said, "Which floor?"

"Oh, I'm just riding."

Then the other passengers looked nervous, like they couldn't wait to get off.

Florrie wondered if her attraction to those elevators related to that baby duckling syndrome where a duckling imprints on whatever it sees first. Her first journey in life, after birth itself, had been riding down to the street in one of those elevators. Of course, she had no delusion that an elevator was her *mother*, but she loved them in a way it would be hard to explain to most people. Today she rode up to twenty, stopped at seven and six on the way down, wondered why no one got on, and walked back into the blinding light.

If you stood at a certain point outside the Nix hospital on the River Walk and stared up at the huge building from a certain angle, the whole thing looked two-dimensional—an optical illusion that was fun to show people, if they had not seen it before. Florrie wondered if Ramsey had ever seen it. With the sky softening into evening, Florrie stared up along the thin line of the Nix, where they had all been born, she and her slightly older brother, True, and their parents, Della and Ruben. She thought, *How did the builders ever build such a sleek brick building right on the edge of the river without it falling in? How did they make it come together at the top?*

She also thought, with intense surprise and pleasure, *I met somebody I want to see again!* It didn't happen every day.

When Florrie appeared at El Viento soon after, she wrapped a fresh white apron around herself and began helping True bus the piled-up tables when it wasn't even her night. "What happened, Florrie?" asked True. "Did the Robert E. Lee Hotel come back into business?"

True was tall and lean, with a wild shock of thick brown hair. People teased him that the aprons wrapped around him twice. Della was chattering warmly with customers, wearing a bright pink-flowered Hawaiian shirt, refilling glasses of iced tea to help the harried waitresses.

Florrie felt fizzy. "Don't you remember when you helped me last week and I said I'd pay you back? This is it!"

"You can't be serious," he said, grimacing. "You want something; you must want something." But she knew he was pleased.

After hauling tubs of plates and glasses to the dishwasher's shelves, even sponging off the large laminated menus, a job that True found disgusting, Florrie sat in a clean booth doing her homework at top speed. She ate a single cheese enchilada with red gravy sauce, no meat. A fussy toddler was whining in a high chair, flicking tortilla chips at his parents. Then Florrie bussed some more tables. This gave True time to eat. He actually smiled at her, wanly. He said, "I wish I hadn't left my homework at home."

At closing time she leaned against the counter, drumming her fingers, waiting for her mother to finish balancing the register so they could all walk home together. Ten P.M. The last slow diners had just checked out.

Florrie said in a low voice, "Mom, I met this really nice guy today. I think I have a crush."

Della said, "Shhh, I'm counting. Tell me later."

So Florrie wandered back over to True, who was swinging his jacket by the door, waiting. He said, "Where did you go today after school? Did you go home? I went to a movie at Rivercenter. It was horrible, everyone died."

"I went to Justin's Ice."

"Thrilling."

Florrie had always felt as if an invisible cord connected their house and the restaurant. Hundreds of times, she and True had carried to-go food home in plastic bags swinging from their wrists. Guacamole chalupas and savory black beans with a little beer thrown into the cooking water (they liked to tell their friends that), and cheese enchiladas and mounds of Mexican cilantro rice. Florrie figured the life of restaurant-running was in her own blood by now. It was in True's, too, though he always said he couldn't wait to be *out of there.*

Della switched off the lights in the front of the restaurant. "Come on, you two," she said.

Walking the six blocks between the restaurant and home, they could hear the train whistles wailing to the south. Mr. Tiffin was sitting by the splashing pink courthouse park fountain, lit up in the dark. Della waved. He leaned forward as if he didn't recognize them.

"Hey Tiffin, it's bedtime!" shouted True.

"True, that's *rude,*" whispered Florrie. "Also, you should call him *Mr.* Tiffin." Mr. Tiffin, a retired librarian with a long white ponytail now, had been their grandfather's good friend. He used to eat at El Viento every night. Now he said he only ate pineapple from a can for dinner, and cottage cheese. He used to draw

Florrie pictures on napkins. Once he had made her a list of all the downtown businesses he remembered that had closed their doors and disappeared. He lived by himself at the Morris Apartments.

A stream of low-riders passed them, pumping out throbs of loud music.

"Crush on who?" said Della.

But True was next to them now. He turned his head to hear Florrie's answer, looking interested.

"Never mind," Florrie said. No way, no *way* would she tell her brother about a crush! She changed the subject rapidly. "Why did Grandpa Hani start a *Mexican* restaurant, anyway? We were beginning this oral history thing in school today and I was wondering, I mean, if you're Lebanese . . ." She matched her pace to Della's—Florrie's mother was the fastest walker she had ever known.

"He said the city had welcomed him so warmly—"

"Who's your crush, Florrie?" True stuck his nose between them.

"But San Antonio already had *hundreds* of Mexican restaurants," said Florrie, ignoring him.

"Didn't have *his*. Anyway, he wanted customers."

"Florrrrrrrrrrrrrie!"

"I think if I were opening a restaurant, I'd start one that didn't exist here already."

True hooted. "Siberian specialties! How about a little Ecuadorian guinea pig café?"

"No, a falafel stand. Downtown. Just wait. I'll start one someday. A tiny menu and a huge clientele."

"Are you serious? Mom, is she serious?"

The cowboy in a motorized wheelchair zoomed past them singing, "Swing Low, Sweet Chariot" at top volume. In the mornings he passed their house going the other direction, singing, "It's a beautiful morning."

Della said softly, "That is the bravest man in this town."

"At least Hani didn't start a McDonald's, thank God," Florrie said. "McDonald's is a fungus on the landscape!" She shouted it into the dark. The cow-boy was far beyond them by now.

Della sighed. It was a little hard to sigh while walking at a sprinter's pace, but she could manage it. "Girl, you are melodramatic."

"I am factual," Florrie said loudly. "And you are an avoidance artist!"

True started jogging to get away from them.

"Crush on who?" Della whispered. "Tell me, baby!"

3 ~ wish

On Florrie's sixteenth birthday on September 2, she made a pineapple upside-down cake for herself. Two birthday cards were standing on the dining room table—one from Ingrid, their next-door neighbor and baby-sitter of early childhood, now ninety-nine. The card and envelope were handwritten in Ingrid's careful, old-fashioned script. There were sixteen crisp one-dollar bills tucked inside it. Next to Ingrid's card stood a bright yellow handmade card from Florrie's friend Zip. Lizzie was going to bring Florrie a tin of her famous oatmeal-pecan cookies to school tomorrow.

Della had carried home a silver baking tray of

enchiladas from the restaurant for a nice family dinner around the table—very rare in their house. Ruben had picked up a bunch of red roses at Mrs. Elizondo's Alameda Flower Shop around the block.

Before eating, Florrie and her father walked over to the Pig House for Florrie's annual birthday photo. They'd been taking her picture in front of the pig every year since she was three. True had his own birthday photo taken at the Alamo, which Florrie thought showed no originality at all.

True's birthday was the day after Florrie's, September 3. Their parents had wanted children for thirteen years, then oddly had two of them within one year. Florrie liked the fact that for twenty-four hours each year, they were the same age.

Ruben wore a navy blue polo shirt and his dark wraparound shades. "So, are you sad today?" Florrie asked him. He was always sad on people's birthdays. *The unrelenting passage of time.*

"Sure I am," he said. "I'm happy for you being sixteen, though. Try not to think about me." For the picture she raised her hands up to try to cup the pig's snout, as she did every year, but she still couldn't reach it.

On Florrie's third birthday, her parents had told her to blow out the candles on her lemon cake and make a secret wish. "Keep your wish inside you," Della had whispered. "Don't say it out loud."

Florrie's eyes had filled with tears. Why couldn't she say it out loud? She had stomped her feet and wailed.

"Okay, let her tell it!" Ruben had said, sighing loudly. "Why not? What difference does it make?"

And Florrie, whose shiny brown hair cascaded down her back in those days, announced as loudly as she could, "I wish! I wish for more *ice cream* like that kind with the *bumpy* things in it named like a street!"

"Rocky Road!" True shouted its name.

Well, it was a good thing Florrie told. Someone had to go buy it for her at the store. You couldn't go shopping for groceries alone when you were *three*.

That day Florrie initiated a new tradition in their household—from then on, people would tell their wishes before blowing out candles. This was usually a good thing for the wisher, since the odds a wish might be fulfilled were substantially increased.

After she got older, Ruben gave Florrie nearly the same gift every year ("So why wrap it?" asked True)—a very nice box of Crane stationery, because he knew she liked to write letters, a stack of Post-it pads in neon hues, and a bundle of blue, thin-tipped Flair marker pens.

True always gave her a gift certificate to the movies.

Della always gave her weird underwear and socks. This year was no exception. Florrie ripped open some strange boxer shorts imprinted with neon yellow ducks. Della grinned. "They're for sleeping in."

Florrie had arranged the pieces of pineapple for her cake topping in a smiley face. She said, "Gather round! Isn't he cute? His expression changed a little when I turned the pan upside down. He looks—*rueful.*"

True snorted. Florrie carefully lit the candles and took a deep breath. "Okay, guys, this year my wish is . . . hey *familia*, everyone listening? My *wish* is that none of you will visit or patronize any franchise establishment for the rest of this calendar year, starting today! That equals sixteen weeks, one week for each year of my life. This will be a *serious project.* We will support independent businesses for all our needs, as much as is possible. Okay? Agreed?"

She took a deep breath, blew, and snuffed the little flickers out.

If there could be silence like a pool of spilled paint.
Silence strung like a clothesline with nothing on it.

Her father got an odd grin on his face, but didn't say anything.

Her mother raised her eyebrows.

"Are you crazy?" True said, raising both arms toward the ceiling. "Making a wish that intrudes on all our lives like that?"

"I've been thinking about it so much for so long!" Florrie marched around the dining room flapping her arms. Her pointed hat slid to the right. She was actually wearing a party hat covered with blue and red stars. "Since Dad and I took that trip to Alabama. No, before that. Since you and I used to walk around the neighborhood with Ingrid or Grandpa Hani and they would point out boarded-up buildings and tell us what they used to be. The Italian grocery store. Remember? Right over there on South Presa? It's *still* boarded up.

Remember how sad Hani would get when another little shop closed down? It's an experiment! Can it even be done anymore? Downtown is turning into a bunch of hotels and nothing else! Tourist stuff! No real stuff! We have to do this: we have no choice!"

Her whole family kept staring at her so she just continued.

"Like, it might be hard if the car breaks down and we need a part or something. Gas might be hard. That little Pakistani gas station with the weird rip-off name just closed, I know. But you could *try* to find something besides Diamond Shamrock. We can make a few exceptions if necessary. But how will we know if we don't try? Just sixteen little weeks. We're a pilot program! You can stand it!"

She was almost shouting by now.

"We sure *do* have a choice," growled True. "Whatever wild idea suits you is suddenly good for us, too? Who do you think you are? I mean, since you don't even drive, how often did you visit Halt'n'Go anyway?"

Florrie just kept right on talking. "No Gap! No Banana Republic. No Denny's or Wendy's or Bed Bath & Beyond—God, what a strange name that is—no Target, no Wal-Mart, no chains! Take off your chains! We'll learn a little more about what it felt like to be alive a hundred years ago. I also wish we would walk everywhere or ride bikes or take the trolley or bus. As much as possible."

"You only get one wish, not two," said True.

Their parents hadn't said anything yet. Out back their gray cat, Napper, stood up straight against the French door and began meowing loudly. Florrie grabbed the sack of cat food out of the bottom kitchen drawer, ran outside, and poured it for him.

Then she ran back in, picked a glossy apple out of the fruit bowl on the dining table, and held it aloft. "Ruben and I got lost on an access road in Corpus Christi last weekend and it was terrifying!

We could have been anywhere. There were no landmarks."

She turned to True. "Can't you live without the Gap for sixteen weeks?"

True was actually not much of a shopper. Had he even *been* to the Gap within the past year? Recently he had been heard complaining to Della that he only had one pair of pants and was getting tired of washing them every two days. But he said, "People in 1900 were *dreaming* about the Gap! If they could be so lucky!"

Della was drumming her fingers on the table, smiling slightly. "But where will we get our groceries? And what about all my produce for the restaurant? And everything else the restaurant needs every day? I don't know about that. Come to think of it, the Zarzamora Street produce vendors I buy from are pretty independent, aren't they?"

"I think it's great," said Ruben. "Let's do it."

True said, "Mom! Dad! Are you trying to be nice to her just because it's her birthday? I don't think anyone should be allowed to make a wish that infringes on the lives of everyone else in the family. Isn't that kind of *bossy*?"

"Stop being a sheep!" said Florrie. Now she was twirling in a circle, her arms out like a propeller. "Stop following the flock! It is time to wander over the hill to find a better meadow."

"I like my meadow! What about Bill Miller's Barbecue?" asked True.

Ruben laughed out loud. True loved their beef sandwiches and lemon meringue pie.

"They're *local*, so you're in luck!" Florrie said, "Oh True, just *try* it. Don't be such a baby. Sixteen weeks isn't much time at all. Just a little old semester."

"Bill Miller's Barbecue is huge," True said. "I think it's all over south Texas now. Isn't it? Florrie, you are such a fake."

Florrie, who didn't even eat meat, couldn't believe they were arguing about barbecue.

"But it's a *local company*, like the grocery store is, so it's okay."

"Look, she's already making exceptions," said True.

Now Ruben was striding around the dining room with his hands up in the air, looking like one of the raggedy street preachers in Travis Park. "I say, let's *all* try it, *absolutely!*" He spoke with such enthusiasm the rest of them felt surprised. He rarely got excited. "It sounds like fun. And Florrie's right. It would be a nice way to honor the past, all the small businesses and stores that are disappearing—"

"We have to save them, Dad!" yelled Florrie. She threw her arms around him.

"Well, we won't. But it's a nice idea."

"My father believed in this, too," said Della, half to herself, running her fingers along the edge of her floral place mat. "We all really believe in this . . . we just do what's easier. . . . "

True stared. Had his entire family been seized by mind control? "But the spirit of one hundred years ago was desperate, you guys! They wanted to be *us*. They wanted to press a button and have something delivered, or order food from their cars. They wanted *cars*! We should be looking forward more than looking back. Why pretend our ancestors had it so good? Who cares about them, anyway?"

Florrie felt a flame burning inside her tongue.

"True, maybe you—don't—care—about—them. They probably didn't care about you, either. They were too busy, like, chopping wood. But we are not doing this for them. *We are doing it for ourselves.* Don't you see? Did you read where Ralph Nader said, 'To the youth of America . . . beware of being trivialized by the commercial culture that tempts you daily.' Did you read that?"

True said, "Gee, I did not."

Ruben said, "Ralph is right. It does. Tempt you. Commercial culture tempts adults just as much."

True said, "So now we're on a first-name basis with Nader?"

"Always have been," Ruben said. "He cares about little guys."

True said, "I care about ease and comfort."

"We could eat at El Viento every night!" Florrie said. "It would qualify."

"Wouldn't that be sweet? Then we could clean all the tables! And don't we eat there all the time already? You're so tyrannical, Florrie. I don't know why you think you have so much power."

Florrie shrugged. "I don't. But it's my *birthday*. Remember?"

She thought of the Mexican floor cleaner she'd bought at a local botanica recently—she loved the labels of their products. This one was called Do As I Say. If you washed your floor with the liquid, anyone who stepped on it would supposedly be in your power. Maybe she should have cleaned the dining room floor before making her wish.

True groaned. He shook his head so hard his thick brown hair fell over his forehead. He said, "In a few hours, my wish will be that everyone forget *your* wish."

"Doesn't count. You can't do that."

"Just wait. You watch me."

Florrie insisted on long handshakes with everyone, in agreement. True held his hand behind his back, crossing his fingers, till Florrie pulled it out, pressed it to her forehead, and kissed it. He was so shocked he gripped her hand as it went up and down, shaking his head *no* the whole time.

Sixteen weeks of no franchises. As much as was possible. *Agreed.*

4 ～ campaign

Florrie's friends expected her to be a little different. She always had been.

In sixth grade Ms. Phillips, her Keystone English teacher, had given her students the assignment to write their life stories in the form of a children's book. Some students added stick figure drawings and some did small paintings in watercolor. Florrie wrote her life story as if it were a fairy tale.

Once there was a girl who lived in an old neighborhood and loved old things in a way that even she could not understand. At the turn of the millennium, she kept wishing it were the previous *millennium.*

She loved Old Ladies, Elderly Men, Old Houses, Old Spoons, Old Books, Old Bowls, Old Maps, Lace Curtains, Antique Bedspreads, Recipes, Remedies, Stories (but not the dumb stories about knights and battles, which did not interest her in the least), Vintage Postcards and Tintype Photographs, Doilies, Velvet Pillows, Black-and-White Movies, Rocking Chairs, and Vintage Toys, and best of all, she loved Old Buildings and Businesses run by Real People. She loved things that were Fading and Disappearing. How could she help protect them in the World?

The girl knew that once they were gone, it would be really hard for them ever to come back and start over again, like some species of Lost Animals. She also noticed that nobody else was talking about this enough. So, in her own mind she decided to become a Protector, a Spokesperson, for things that were being wrecked and erased in the world, by Big Business Corporations, Urban Development, and basically People with Too Many Dollar Bills.

It would be a Long Road. It would be more like an

Endless Journey among destructionists who put up lying signs—MAKING WAY FOR PROGRESS—when they wreck wonderful buildings, as if to trick us. But we are Not Imbeciles. Once you find out what you care about in life, you have No Choice. You have to work for it.

What if you love a Tree? A Crane? What if you would prefer to pay close attention to Screech Owls rather than to Human Beings? What if you decide to work on behalf of all Seven-year-olds with Cancer or Attention Deficit Disorder? You have to find some Job To Connect To What You Love."

Ms. Phillips wrote, "A little scattered" in the upper right-hand corner but read Florrie's essay out loud to the class. She always did that with at least three of her students' papers. She said Florrie's burst of passion was original and admirable and wished her luck in her mission. She also suggested Florrie consider studying German someday since she seemed to have such a strong affection for the Capital Letter, along with everything else.

A girl named Beth had passed Florrie a note. "I'll work with you" was all it said, with a lavish heart drawn on it, signed "B."

Florrie's friend Zip said her convictions made him feel a little embarrassed about his own story. He had described the life of an armadillo in the Texas hill country who decides to wear a baseball cap but can't find one small enough to fit.

One of her classmates stole a MAKING WAY FOR PROGRESS sign from a construction site (very uncharacteristic behavior for a Keystone student, said Ms. Phillips) and gave it to Florrie all wrapped up, because she hated it so much.

So, years later, extending the project from her family to her classmates didn't seem like such a far-fetched thing to do.

The day after her birthday, Florrie tacked up posters on the bulletin board in the lunchroom calling for a "Meeting of the Minds." Then she took them down. That sounded too much like work. School was already work. She had to make this sound like an adventure.

ARE YOU INDEPENDENT?
EXPERIMENT WITH US!
SUPPORT INDEPENDENT ENTERPRISE
IN SAN ANTONIO!
MEET ON GRASS OUTSIDE THEATER
AT 3:15 THURSDAY FOR 15 MINUTES
THAT COULD CHANGE YOUR LIFE!!!!!!!

A day later Florrie and Zip were sitting in the sun at the outdoor concrete tables at school after lunch. "I don't want to speak at the meeting," Zip said, groaning. "Please don't make me speak. You speak."

"Oh come on!" Florrie said, giving him a nudge. "You're not shy. The anteater wants you to."

Years ago someone had sketched an R-rated anteater in the wet concrete sidewalk across the street from the school. People often blamed things on him.

"It's not a matter of shyness, Florrie. No. I drink slushies from Sonic. I *enjoy* going to the mall. It would be fake for me to speak."

"Please, Zip? Can't you turn over a new leaf for a while? Just a temporary one?"

"I like my leaves."

"You remind me of my brother."

"He's a cool guy."

Zip ran a hand through his messy blond hair. Florrie enjoyed doing this herself when she was in a better mood with him. He shrugged his shoulders and stared at her. "Okay, I'll think of something."

In seventh grade they had danced together at the Spring Dance and kissed behind the bleachers in the gym. Back in the secret cavern of lost gym shoes and empty soda cups, she had felt her lips wake up for the first time. What had these lips been doing all these years? Zip smelled slightly minty, a comforting toothpaste clean.

Now and then a father-chaperone would appear

alongside the bleachers clicking his fingers, "*Hello in there*, come on back to the dance floor please!" and they would scuttle forth from the shadows to rejoin the crowd.

In eighth grade Zip and Florrie had every class together. Although Keystone was a very small school (only thirty-eight students in their grade), Zip acted as if this were a heavenly sign. It made his life easier when he didn't copy his homework assignments accurately—*rrrrrrrring!* went Florrie's phone. She answered saying, "Math? Or History?"

Zip could always make Florrie laugh. Once in ninth grade, they had walked all the way from school down to the San Fernando Cathedral, nearly to Florrie's house, to visit the vault which supposedly contained Davy Crockett's bones.

"Did I ever tell you I used to kneel here?" Zip had asked. "When I was little, I prayed to Davy Crockett. He was my secret guardian angel. I wanted one of those hair-tails so I could look like him without the coonskin hat. When my mother found out, she was horrified and started dragging me over to the Virgin Mary."

Zip ran his finger across Florrie's smooth forehead. "You are one pretty girl," he said.

Florrie shook her head. He still seemed to think of her as his girlfriend sometimes; he'd never really had another one.

"I'm tired of ideas," he said. "Let's talk about something petty and personal—like, me. You, and me. You want to go bowling this Friday night? Lizzie and Bailey want to go."

Florrie shook her finger at him. "Maybe. We're talking about something else right now."

"But what will I say?"

"You will urge everyone to try an experiment. That's how my dad says we should describe it. Don't make it seem like drudgery. Make it seem like an adventure. When's the last time you ate at Luther's or Olgita's Gorditas?"

Olgita's served some of the best chips and warm homemade salsa in town.

"Uh—yesterday."

"See! You're already part of the movement."

"Movement? Don't say 'movement'!"

"Oh please! When you talk, you could just give contrasts. Say, for example, if you eat at Long John Sicko, you know what you'll get. It is not interesting. Not to mention not healthy. It is *corporate America.* The people who work there will never know your name."

"Do I *want* them to know my name? Hey, I know what I'll get at Olgita's too! I always order the avocado chalupas."

"And doesn't it taste like somebody's grandmother's cooking?"

He stared at her. She really seemed to have an obsession for old ladies.

Their friend Juan passed by flicking his fingers at them.

Zip mouthed to Juan, "Save me!" Three sparrows twittered around a bush.

"Juan, I want to talk to you," Florrie said.

"Okay, after history. I'm late to turn something in." He waved a sheaf of papers and kept walking.

Florrie went on to Zip. "Does Taco Smell taste like somebody's grandmother?"

"It tastes like somebody's Styrofoam."

"Okay! Say it! I'm asking two other people to talk and you are going to be first. I will introduce the subject, then you'll talk."

"Why?"

"You have a good normal personality."

"And you don't?"

Florrie grinned at him. "Well, it's my idea. So you need to be my supporter. Supporters *talk*."

At three-twenty Bailey, Juan, Lizzie, Zip, and Beth were sitting on the grass by the steps to the theater. True sat nearby on a stone wall. He stared at them for a minute, then lowered his head to his notebook as if he were going to *study*. He had to wait for Florrie since they rode home together.

Florrie was nervous, dashing among her friends,

leaning over to pat them on their shoulders. She was wearing gray cargo pants and a T-shirt imprinted with pale gray waves. Finally she settled down beneath the pecan tree, crossed her legs, and began to speak. "Hey guys. I love you for coming. Are you curious what this is about? Here's the thing. I'm worried. For San Antonio and for the whole United States—our cities and towns are losing their flavor with all these same disgusting franchises taking over everywhere."

Bailey raised his eyebrows. Beth picked at a pouf of dried grasses by the fence, nodding her head at appropriate moments. Florrie continued, "I've been thinking about this subject for *years.* Almost since I was born, and the situation sure is not getting better. I think it's time to do something, and I've thought of something we can do."

Beth looked up. Juan cleared his throat. Two sparrows landed on the trash Dumpster and gazed at each other. Was that where they went for dates?

"It's really hard for someone to start a small

business these days, the way our ancestors did, and make it last. You know? Little businesses shut down all the time. I mean, it's unbelievable what's disappeared in our city." They'd heard this from her before. Here and there. Random remarks. Everyone was now listening to her dutifully. Florrie's low voice gained in ferocity as she went on.

"Do you think this is irrelevant? I realize you may just be trying to finish your homework. You may be focusing on getting into college and who wants more to think about? But I am really *really* worried about our world. I think more people should be worried.

"And I thought we might try an *experiment*, you know, to see if a small group of people can still be heard . . . so I enlisted my family first, and everyone in my family agreed"—in her peripheral vision she could feel True's head shoot up as he glared at her—"but right away, it seemed to me the experiment would be better with more people participating. This is where you come in. The deal is—avoid all franchises for the rest of this year. Sixteen weeks. A semester. Support independent businesses as much as you can. Keep a list of where you go and maybe where you don't go. Encourage other people you know to do it, too. It will be fun. We need you! Zip will speak first!"

Zip gulped and adjusted his shirt. Now what was he supposed to say?

"Well, Florrie and I have been talking. About some of these . . . umm . . . issues . . . little guys . . . umm . . . having a really hard time. You know? Like, closing down. Florrie thinks Wal-Mart is the devil. Did you know in Mexico it's called Wal-Mex? Weird. Did you hear about the Wal-Mart in Boerne that fired a worker for wearing an Arab headdress and a priest's collar and like a whole lot of crosses, saying he was trying to bring religions together? Anyway, we were going to suggest that you stop going to—umm—less original places like McDonald's and Wendy's and Taco Bell—umm—do you *go* there?—sure you do—also clothes and music chains, if you know what I mean, and if you stop going there, you will discover better places right under your nose. I mean, like, look around."

Their history teacher, Mr. Humble, had stopped near where they sat and cocked his head. "Hey guys, making history?" It was what he always said.

"You wanna join us?" asked Lizzie. "You'd like this idea!"

"Love to, but on the way to meet with my brethren teachers," he said, waving. Mr. Humble's class had recently been talking about the United States in 1905, when some Americans were worried about "loss of individualism" and "growing corporate power." Florrie had highlighted all those sections in her text.

Zip continued, "If we support the true— umm—independent—business persons of our community—they will be able—to buy better cars. Just kidding. They deserve our support. If we don't support them, uh, they might shut down. I mean, we need to like put our money where it counts, know what I mean? Not that we have much money. Because if they shut, our city would lose its—uh—flavor." He paused, then continued in a last rush. "Dudes, we would like you to be part of this—campaign! In fact, Juan is going-totalktoyouaboutwhatyoucandorightnow."

He said these last words as if he had been struck by lightning, then rolled over into a fetal position.

Florrie leaned over and patted his ear. Maybe he needed to take a class in public speaking.

Juan pulled a file folder from his backpack. He wore a Radiohead T-shirt and khaki pants with red paint streaked down one leg. He shook his beautiful black hair out of one eye. Florrie felt amazed she had gotten him to agree to this. Juan was very shy.

"Yeah, I am the poster man," he said softly. He waved some eight-by-eleven sheets of colored paper. "I was thinking, we make some nice, *artistic* little posters, maybe the business places that—you know—hang loose—would post them for us. If we said in the posters to the customers, something like 'Congratulations for Supporting a Real Place in Our Town'—as opposed to—someplace that's in *every* town, we might help people think about it."

Lizzie, who had recently taken to wearing pastel flower-print skirts and blond dreadlocks, said, "So the posters would be congratulating *us*? Don't you think the posters should be congratulating *them*? Like, bravo to *you* for being independent? Won't it be harder to get people to hang up posters congratulating *us*?"

"Good point," said Florrie.

Zip coughed. "I think they should congratulate *everyone*. Go both ways. Like, we're smart because we shopped there. You're smart because you found a way to stay open with all the—umm—greedy giants surrounding you. Everybody's smart."

Bailey laughed loudly. He was doodling on his Spanish book cover, making small, round-topped buildings with tall towers coming out of them. "Florrie," he said, "you're a 1960s kind of girl."

"Stop it," Florrie said, snapping her fingers in front of his face.

But he continued. "We're lazy now. Change the channel! Something bothers us? We go, *Oh well. Call out the military.* We're used to being entertained. Has anyone you know in this school ever been to a demonstration?" Bailey asked.

Florrie said, "Sure!"

He looked surprised.

"I went to that anti-death-penalty march last fall," said Juan.

"I always go to peace rallies with my dad. Don't you guys march in the Martin Luther King parade every year? I went to the Million Mom March without my mom," Florrie said.

"I'm impressed." Bailey looked around.

Lizzie said, "I went to it, too."

Bailey said, "Okay, forget it. You guys do more than I do. I'll be the secretary for the meeting. These are my minutes." He held up his doodles and smiled.

Juan looked hesitant, but continued. "Excuse me, do I have to make *all* the posters? Could everybody design one and I'll get the copies made and give them back to you all and then we all post them?" He passed around sheets of paper before anyone could say no.

"But wait, guys," said Florrie. "We need to *agree* on the pact together first. Does everyone promise that you will boycott franchises as much as possible *yourselves*?"

Zip often stopped at McDonald's on the way home from school. Lizzie's brother worked at Dairy Queen. She usually had a chocolate milkshake when she went to pick him up.

"My sister is heavily into deprivation!" True called out. It was his first contribution to the dialogue.

But Bailey pulled through. "Old Navy and Target are like oxygen or what? We can live without them!"

Florrie had the feeling some people were grimacing or frowning when she blinked.

"Florrie, maybe you should go live in Mexico or France someday—don't they still have lots of little shops there?" Lizzie said.

Fat gray doves were cooing on the drainpipe above their heads. Lizzie blew a kiss at them. "Hey birdy-birdies."

"We need to make it sound *fun* so people will do it," Florrie said.

True snorted. "*That* won't be easy."

Florrie ignored him. "Make it sound like—a way to discover our true city. Spread this word among our friends. So it feels more like a wave." Zip ran his finger along the pale gray wave pattern on her shoulder. Florrie continued. "I think we should have a rally downtown to kick it off. Don't you?" Beth was nodding vigorously now. She liked gatherings. She could bring her guitar.

"Bailey, could you call the newspaper to try to get a reporter there?" Florrie continued. "I'll give you the number to call. I can't call myself, because of my dad. Also, some of us should write letters to the editor saying we need special places or our city won't be special anymore. Again, I can't do it because of my dad. But I could write to the *Current!*"

The *Current* was the alternative newspaper in town.

"And I'll get Daniel involved! He'll love it," said Lizzie. "And Amon in my Spanish class seems like the type. And what about teachers? I *know* Mr. Humble would be interested because he told us he had a personal vendetta against some big store for some reason, like, they wouldn't take back the rotten lawn mower he bought there and he got really mad."

"Teachers, coaches, mail carriers—anyone," said Florrie. "We're just the core group. What if our campaign could spread citywide?"

"The Café Latino would be really crowded," said Bailey.

They loved to go to the Café Latino for chess night to drink mocha iced coffees with fresh

"You know how Dad asked me to clean the tool-shed? Groan. I need to organize it. So I saw this heap of boxes behind the counter. The lady saw me staring at them and offered them to me. I didn't even ask."

"See! Little places notice people!" Florrie patted his arm.

He snorted. "Maybe I'll invite her to come help clean the toolshed."

5 ~ potato enchiladas

For the next few days, after school and on the weekend, Florrie's friends dutifully carried rainbow stacks of posters all over town. Some shopkeepers and restaurant owners understood immediately when the students described what they were doing. They seemed grateful to hear of such a campaign.

Others appeared perplexed, even when Florrie and her friends took pains to describe the project carefully. Were they selling something? Were they casing the joint for a future burglary?

Everyone kept lists of places that said yes to hanging the posters. Florrie's places were:

Tienda Guadalupe and San Angel, two great folk arts stores; Segovia's Mexican Candies, fresh pecan pralines stacked by the cash register; Karam's Restaurant, a Mexican restaurant on the west side of town, run by another Lebanese family, with a mysterious "Mayan Garden" out back—palm trees, twining vines, and giant floodlit carved heads; and The Liberty Bar, with its crooked wooden floors, homemade breads lined on a long table, and geranium pudding.

The New and Old Shop was happy for a poster (Florrie couldn't resist buying a hand-stitched pillowcase while she was in there, and a set of 1920s Japanese children's magazines), as was El Mirador, one of El Viento's downtown competitors, serving famous soups and unusual entrees. Florrie liked to go there during the summers and sit outside between the banana palms, under the ceiling fans. She had once told Della, "I don't think our menu has a single item that stands up to El Mirador's potato enchiladas," and Della got quiet for the whole evening.

Posters also went up at Paris Hatters, Gini's Home Cooking, Twin Sisters, Teka Molino, offering "bean cups" that looked like bonnets for mice, and Madhatters Tea.

Lizzie hung one at Schilo's Delicatessen: "Since 1917," homemade-in-a-barrel root beer (free refills from a frosty pitcher), tall wooden booths, and German pea soup. Zip and Bailey ran into each other at Hogwild, the independent music store. Zip described his "extreme good luck" on a single two-block stretch of South Flores Street. "Check it out." He showed Florrie his list. "Gordo's Café, Mary Lou's Café, Mommy & Me Flower Shop—personally I'd change the name—and Botanica Eloise. Oh yeah, also the Land of Oldies."

"Oldies?"

"Records. One million of them. Didn't you wonder where they'd all gone? All kinds of music jammed in this little bitty shop. Cool place."

Juan had swooped to the southeast side of the city, where he hung a poster at Mr. & Mrs. G's and ate two pieces of buttermilk pie, which he had never tasted before in his life.

But Florrie had a problem with her own mother after creating a special giant lime green sign for El Viento on two full-size poster boards.

Della objected to filling the entire front picture window of the restaurant with it.

"*Mija*, it will take up all our light!"

"But you have so much business; there is *huge* foot traffic on this street. And *you are my mother*! We want to spread the word."

"Why, baby? What good will that do for you?"

"Don't you care if you have customers or not?"

"Of course I do. But I'm packed already! Business is great."

"You're lucky, Mom! Not everyone else is so lucky. Do you know how many little restaurants closed last year?"

"Probably the same number as new ones that opened."

"Wrong! Franchises opened! You know that!"

"Honey, I like those little posters better. You can hang two of them, but leave light in between, okay? I'll go crazy if it's dark at the checkout."

"Let me hang three?" Florrie asked.

"Two!"

"I can't believe you're so unsupportive! We're doing this for *you*!"

Florrie went back to the stockroom and dipped a white kitchen towel in cool water over the giant sink and squeezed it out.

She flopped down on the cot that had been hers since she was a little girl. Actually, it had been her mother's, too, when her mother was a girl. She placed the towel across her eyes.

Advocacy was exhausting.

When your family had a restaurant, you knew the bathroom mirror as well as you knew your own at home. You knew the slightly delayed flush of the toilet and the distinctive clicks of the locks. You knew what the cheese looked like in a Giant Block.

Florrie took a deep breath and tried to picture a pool of blue water inside her mind, with layers of ripples extending outward from one pitched-in stone. That stone held all her tiredness. The stone held fussy words and worry and the school assignments she knew she should have started by now.

She took a deep breath and felt calmer. Then she conjured up three pleasant mental images: their cat, Napper, stretched on the wooden deck snoozing in the sun; their neighbor Ingrid wearing a huge pink package bow on her head on Easter; and the crisp salad piled on top of the potato enchiladas at El Mirador. Florrie sat up, pulled Grandpa Hani's gray cashmere sweater, which still smelled like his Canoe cologne, off its hook, and lay down again, covering herself with it.

Florrie's whole family kept changes of clothing and extra shoes in the back room at the restaurant, along with the mop and the bucket on wheels and the plump packages of one thousand white napkins. Since Florrie maintained an allegiance to only gray clothing, everyone could tell which garments were hers.

Florrie had adopted the all-gray policy on her thirteenth birthday after seeing a painting called *Two Grays* by Ellsworth Kelly at the museum. She packed or gave away every clothing item she owned that was brightly hued, patterned, or striped. To fill in the gaps, she shopped at the Salvation Army and the Green Door, purchasing a baggy gray jacket that looked like an old painter's coat, three pairs of gray pants, and four T-shirts with long and short gray sleeves. She had a gray jumper and a gray skirt.

Florrie loved how different grays looked side by side, like a calm palette at the paint store. Fog. Mist. The color of lakes in winter. The tint of undecided sky. Neutral clothes were empowering. They let you fade into any scene. Florrie felt unobtrusive wearing them. She even wore gray socks and gray shoes. She wore an antique engraved silver bracelet with a turquoise stone. It looked excellent with gray.

True teased Florrie, of course. He asked her at least once a month if she were a Mennonite.

She said, "Do Mennonites wear gray? They do not. Some wear old-fashioned clothes, but many don't. The Mennonite church is right down the block. They are also pacifists and care about their communities. Maybe I *will* join them. Hey, feel free to wear your same tattered blue jeans for the next twenty years and I won't mention them, okay?"

Florrie's father felt a kinship with her favorite color. Gray matched his usual gloomy mood. He had secretly considered being the second in their family to go gray, but thought he would never hear the end of it from Della, who favored Hawaiian getups and madly stitched peasant shirts. Florrie's mother bought her clothing "gently used" from Operation Friendship. She thought happy clothing made people feel happier, the way holiday cards taped to the cash register at the restaurant made people feel festive. The way a burst of sunflowers lit up a field.

6 ～ changing fountains park

Florrie selected the courthouse park with its little changing-colors fountain for the rally. The park was in front of San Fernando Cathedral. Lots of people passed by there on foot. A vendor under an umbrella sold candy-colored *raspas* and Mexican snacks. Friday afternoon would be a bustling, visible time.

"A rally?" asked True, when she told him about her plan at dinner (cheese and avocado and pickle sandwiches this time, slathered with mayonnaise). "Is this a political party now?"

"People have *pep* rallies for lesser things every day of the week," answered Florrie, shoving an apple—dessert—at his stomach.

Later she started thinking of the gathering more as a "wake-up call."

Florrie and her friends had canvassed their neighborhoods, sticking neon pink notes in people's mailboxes and under their doors. They stuffed notes into lockers and posted them in the cafeteria and on the hall's announcement boards: PLEASE STAND UP FOR OUR CITY! RALLY ON SEPTEMBER 26, 5:30 P.M.

Lizzie said Mr. Humble had promised to attend. The Spanish teacher, Ms. Bella Luna, said she'd try to come. Beth asked if they wanted her to write a song for the day. Or should she just sing Joni Mitchell's "Parking Lot"?

The twins in Florrie's art class said they would attend if she gave them gift certificates to El Viento to spend later. She was wide-eyed. Bribery?

On September 26 Florrie rode her green one-speed bike down to the courthouse park an hour early. Her rally poster, printed in red on giant brown

paper—WE LOVE INDEPENDENT BUSINESSES!—
was rolled in her basket. She chained her bike to a
NO PARKING FROM HERE TO CORNER sign at the
park, and began pacing.

She'd been too nervous to do any homework
after school and found herself making a few last-
minute calls—to her mother's friend Chrissie,
owner of Sea Island, the best seafood restaurant in
town for thirty years, and her Uncle Joaquin, who
ran a dusty, wonderful shoe repair shop on the
west side of town. "You're doing what?" he said.
He didn't quite get it, but he couldn't leave the
shop anyway.

Florrie had also called her parents to remind
them. Her mother's voice sounded strained. Two
waitresses had quit that morning after a fight with
the cook. "I'll do my best, baby," she groaned.
"But it's really wild over here." Ruben was on a
deadline and didn't answer the phone at his desk.

In the park a refreshing wind was lifting the
leaves. San Antonians waited with great anticipa-

tion for the first hints of autumn after the long summer. A homeless woman with a knapsack and a cane sat on a rolled blue blanket next to the fountain, staring at Florrie with mild interest. Florrie nodded at her. She saw Zip circling the park in his battered station wagon, honking and waving. He was looking for a parking meter. Bailey, Lizzie, and Beth were with him.

The others to arrive early were the Martino brothers, two middle-aged men from Florrie's neighborhood whose grandmother had been a founder of the Conservation Society. They each carried large posters on poles: SUPPORT LITTLE BUSINESSES IN SAN ANTONIO! and KEEP SAN ANTONIO UNIQUE! This pleased Florrie immensely. She had said, "Hi, how's it going?" to these men all her life, but never had an in-depth conversation with them till the evening she stopped by their neat, flowery yard to invite them to the rally.

Ingrid, Florrie and True's old babysitter, came, of

course, walking very slowly from the trolley stop, wearing a frilly pink Easter bonnet from 1943. Florrie had made her sign, SAY NO TO FRANCHISES!, which she was holding proudly.

Mr. Tiffin surprised Florrie by appearing with a large, folded parachute, which seemed very strange. Parachute strings were dangling down. He seemed in danger of tripping on them. "Who's the dude who just landed?" Zip whispered to Florrie. Which indeed, paralleled Mr. Tiffin's sign, visible when he spun the parachute around the other way: BEWARE!!!! FRANCHISES ARE LANDING ON OUR HEADS EVERY DAY. Florrie laughed out loud.

Angela, who ran a movie rental shop called Planet of the Tapes, appeared at the park in a serape, pushing her baby, Wiley Francisco, in a stroller. Her sign said, SUPPORT RESIDENTS AS MUCH AS TOURISTS! Three ladies from Florrie's neighborhood appeared with big dogs on leashes. Wiley tried to grab their tails. Florrie felt deeply touched that her own neighborhood was showing up. And there was Mr. Humble, with his trumpet! Beth had asked him to bring it. He was going to play a few bars to catch everyone's attention.

Florrie kept checking her watch (a kid's watch with spiders and lizards on a purple band) to make sure she began speaking exactly at 5:30, no matter how many people had arrived. Zip had borrowed a megaphone from the school coach. It said "Keystone Cobras" on it.

She was surprised when True jogged up at the last minute, breathless, a button-down shirt slung over his shoulder. "I have a message for you from Dad. Would you *please* get a cell phone?" Florrie and her father didn't like cell phones. They liked phones connected to walls. "He says he can't come over here. Mom called him all upset, and he's actually going to the restaurant to be a waitress for a while, as am I. Some of us have to *work*. They're doing a boat dinner tonight for one of the Spurs. They're going crazy."

"Which Spur?"

"I do not know. Have fun. We won't. Can you come over there when you're finished?"

A huge wind roared in, rattling the trees. *The first cooling day.* Florrie stared up. Was this a good omen? A Texas norther could make the temperature plummet twenty degrees in an hour. Signs began to flutter and flap.

Lizzie, who was wearing a yellow tank top with "Love" on it in Hebrew, Arabic, and English, said, "I wish I'd worn sleeves!"

Florrie's neighbor Lucy, who apparently stayed tuned to the Weather Channel at all hours, tried to hand a red cardigan sweater to Lizzie, but Lizzie declined it. It wasn't very stylish. She didn't want to put it on.

Beth was singing to a TV camera no one had noticed before. Florrie heard her croon the word "little, little, little" like a chant. Would they really put that on TV?

Florrie's friends from art class stood slouched among the palms in faded black, sheens of ripped and raveled black. They turned north and south with their signs, grinning sheepishly. Florrie wove in and out of the group, trying to introduce people. Streams of workers had begun exiting the courthouse across the street. A few turned their heads for a quick glance. Juan extended his arm to offer them flyers. A few people accepted them. Some tourists waiting for their bus had straggled over from the cathedral's coffee shop. Florrie passed around lime green "SUPPORT INDEPENDENT BUSINESSES IN OUR CITY!" handouts with good graphics by Juan and coupons for 30 percent off at a long list of places. That should get people's attention!

El Viento topped the list. Mi Tierra, a popular Mexican restaurant open twenty-four hours a day, with Christmas lights strung up year-round, offered 30 percent off on all bakery items.

Florrie picked up the megaphone and took a deep breath.

A rancher in a white cowboy hat waiting to cross

the street paused to stare at them. "Is this against abortion?" he said, squinting.

Florrie said, "No, it's against franchises." He looked perplexed.

Maybe he was from Three Rivers or Pleasanton, small towns south of San Antonio. She should have invited him to pick up a sign and stand beside her. How many little enterprises did his own community have left? Western wear, cattle feed, rope . . .

She said, "Independent businesses need our support!"

And he shrugged.

He just shrugged and crossed the street.

He didn't say, "You're right!" and salute her.

He didn't say, "You're wrong!"

He just shrugged as if to say "So?", which seemed to Florrie a true insult.

She couldn't even argue with him.

The trumpet flared. Everyone stopped chatting. "THANK YOU FOR COMING!" Florrie's voice, in the wind, through the megaphone, sounded distorted and huge. "WE NEED YOU! WE NEED EVERY ONE OF YOU! PLEASE TRY OUR EXPERIMENT! PLEASE BOYCOTT ALL LARGE FRANCHISE BUSINESSES AS MUCH AS YOU CAN! We're trying for sixteen weeks. San Antonio is lucky to have some little businesses left. Please support them. We need to make a strong effort and tell our friends! PASS IT ON! We've been going around putting posters in independent businesses to thank them for staying alive. I mean, anything you can think of doing . . . "

Someone called out, "What about groceries?"

Florrie said, "Local chains are okay! But check out all the farmers' markets, too!"

The TV camera trained on her made her feel self-conscious. She tried to ignore it.

"We urge you to write letters to the editor and speak out in your churches and synagogues and mosques and wherever—and your clubs and schools and neighborhoods. Keep spreading the word! Avoid franchises with all your might! It's hard, because they're everywhere. But it's also— simple! Try to notice how many little businesses there still are and go to them. Explore the city. Check out the backstreets!" Florrie felt a little dizzy. Maybe she should have written down notes in advance. "AGAIN, THANK YOU FOR CARING! DOES ANYONE HAVE ANY QUESTIONS?"

A guy from the courthouse raised his hand and Florrie passed him the megaphone. (This could be dangerous, she realized. Who knew what someone else would say?)

He said, "Hi!"—jumping back from the sound of his own enlarged voice. He was cute, and young, and his blue tie, at the end of a workday, was crooked and loose around his neck.

He said again, "Uh, I have no idea who any of you are or anything, but I live out on Bandera Road—and if any of you want to see franchises, come on out. We're in trouble, man. The traffic is *unbelievable*! What you are doing sounds good to me!"

He passed the megaphone back and nodded as people clapped.

Florrie said, "Thank you! Move downtown! Anyone else?"

No other hands went up.

Florrie said, "Okay, this is Beth, who's going to sing for us!"

Beth, with her gentle voice, could really have used a microphone. But the megaphone was all they had. No one could understand her soft words, except the last line, which she repeated more loudly, "We won't forget, forget, forget."

Then people drifted in circles, chatting, handing coupons around to pedestrians passing by.

A TV reporter jumped down from a TV truck that had pulled up in a loading zone. He chatted with the cameraman for a moment, looked around, and shouted, "Who's in charge?"

Everyone pointed at Florrie.

"Your campaign," said the reporter, after she spelled her name, "seems absolutely idealistic."

"Sure it is," said Florrie. The wind was blowing ferociously now. She had to speak at a louder-than-usual volume.

The reporter had silver wire-rim glasses and shaggy salt-and-pepper hair. He continued, "In an almost 1960s kind of way."

"Was that the only decade in which people were allowed to be idealistic? I don't think so," said Florrie.

"Do you really think a small campaign like this could have any effect at all?"

"Why not? Everything starts small!" (What was that Margaret Mead quote she had read? She should have brought it.) "Awareness of a problem is a first step toward solving it. Just to make people *think* about where they shop and eat and—who they support. We want to make them think twice! Think three times! I mean—at this point we're just a little group of *teens*, most of us don't really have much money to *spend* yet, but maybe we'll think about things differently . . . as we get older and have more money. Maybe we'll be more careful about where we . . . shop and eat, you know? Making our choices. Does America still feel like it has any? Umm . . . we'll think *hard* before we support those giant places that have nothing to do, really, with our own communities, you know."

Florrie absolutely hated lapsing into "umms" and "you knows" but it was hard to feel fluent when a reporter stared at you dubiously from close range and pointed a microphone or a camera at your mouth.

She gulped. *Try to do better.*

He said, "Well, just to be a devil's advocate, the megastores do offer *jobs* to our community."

"Yes, well, so did every other smaller enterprise."

"But what about prices? Large stores offer cheaper prices due to mass quantity buying. . . ."

"We lose more than we gain."

That phrase just popped out of her mouth. She liked it. She'd have to remember it.

Florrie said, "Think about what's vanished, just from downtown alone! My grandpa and mom and dad are always pointing out where special places used to be. Rosengren's Books. Norman Brock's Books where they had a million used books up to the ceiling! The Manhattan Restaurant—and what do we get instead? Some stupid chain!" Then she thought, *Be positive. Engage your listeners.* This was not live coverage. They would edit the tape back at the studio. So she said in a softer tone, "Did you ever love any place—that went away?"

The reporter was looking thoughtful now, as if something she said had clicked with him. Instead of answering, he asked a different kind of question. "What if hundreds of people did what you are doing? Or hundreds of thousands? Say— a *week* of supporting independent establishments—every year around Independence Day? It might catch on. Or what about a week at

Thanksgiving—being thankful for whatever little enterprises are left. Or what about . . . a week every other *month*, say. As a practice. A kind of devotion, say. Would you go for that?"

A kind of devotion? Florrie noted the phrase. She was liking this reporter more and more by the second.

"Yes!" she said. "I sure would!"

When he asked, "Tell me again, how long is your campaign?" she said, "Sixteen weeks. Well, to make it easier, you could just say till the end of this year."

The interview ended there.

Florrie saw one of the lime green coupon pages discarded in the street. Someone had accepted it and thrown it down? Maybe it had blown loose from someone's hand. She picked it up and smoothed it out.

Afterward, as people dispersed (Tiffin wrapping himself in the parachute to walk home, nodding and murmuring "Good job, Florrie, good job"), Florrie's friends suggested they all wander a few blocks north to El Viento and have dinner together. This caught her off guard. "Uh, I don't think it's a good night over there. Hmm—how about let's go to Acenar?" She felt a little guilty and sat with her friends out on the balcony at Acenar, a block from her family's place.

They all munched hot chips dipped in fresh salsa and talked about how the rally had gone. Bailey was distracted by a reference Mr. Humble had made to a recent history test. "I'm afraid it will set you back," he'd said. "Did he say anything like that to the rest of you guys?" Bailey asked. "Does that mean I flunked?"

Beth said, "Florrie, I liked that old lady Lucy from your neighborhood. Did you see her keep giving the V sign to the camera?"

Lizzie said, "La Fonda's not a chain, is it?"

Later, after Zip dropped her off at home, Florrie fell asleep on the couch in front of the TV and missed the news report. She couldn't believe she had done that. Shortly afterward she woke when her grumpy family came in.

"How was it?" her parents asked.

At least her dad said, "I'm sad to have missed it."

The next day her friends told her the news report looked great.

7 ~ pigeons

If you give someone your phone number, then you wonder whether or not they are *ever* going to call you. If you are not home when they call, will someone else in your family pick up the phone and forget to tell you about it, or if they hear the message on the machine before you do, will they erase it by mistake or play it repeatedly, making fun of it? "Ramsey? Who's Ramsey? Anybody ever hear of anyone named Ramsey?"

That was why Florrie thought e-mail might be preferable to phoning. Thank goodness she had given her e-address to Ramsey, too. She didn't have to be home if he wanted to make contact (what was his problem?) and he could say whatever he wanted without his message being possible public information. The only bad part was, Florrie was now checking her e-mail nine times a day to see if he had written, which was quite an interruption. What was it they called that disorder? OCD?

And why hadn't she gotten his data, anyway? She didn't even know his last name.

She thought of him while working at the restaurant. Enchiladas verdes. Chalupas compuesta. Puffy tacos with rice. Fish Vera Cruz, spiky tomato sauce, fragrant and steaming. After meeting Ramsey and not hearing from him again for a week, Florrie thought she might vaporize like steam over the giant pot of tortilla soup. It was really pathetic, that someone you didn't even know could have so much power over you.

She wished he would walk in.

Zip walked in instead, wearing a bright yellow baseball cap. Zip, who was avoiding franchises with all his might to make her happy. He had even given up his Dairy Queen banana splits and had discovered two foreign film series programs at local universities he might otherwise have missed. He was raving about films from Iran and Turkey. "You should have been with me, Florrie! You should be with me *all the time*!" He hugged her tightly.

"Oh Zip," she said, pulling back. "You are so nice to me. Why are you so nice?"

He grinned. "Am I? It smells good in here. I could live in this restaurant."

"Some of us do," said Florrie. "There's a cot in the back, by the way. Have you ever seen it? Clothes and combs and stuff."

"If I run away, I'm coming here."

Late that night when Florrie checked her e-mail for the last time before bed, she saw an unfamiliar address in her in-box. It did not look like one of those penis enlargement maniacs or Nigerians desperate to share their wealth, so she clicked in to read:

Hey remember me?
I'm the guy you ate kiwi beside at the river.
Sorry it took me so long to make contact but
I lost your phone and e-address.
It turned up though. How's it going?
Wanna take a walk?
Go see why all the pigeons live outside the
Alpha Hotel?
Speak to me.

Ramsey

8 ~ on the mission trail

Ramsey wanted to see everything: the toilet seat museum, the Shrine of the Black Madonna. He wanted to see the wolf-dog spirit that supposedly haunted the grounds of Mission Espada. Florrie had never heard of it, despite her specialization in Weird Things.

She was more than willing to ride her bicycle alongside him to get to the missions, especially since he wanted to leave very early on a Sunday, when there would be no traffic and they could ride down the centers of the streets. This meant he had to leave his own house in Alamo Heights about five A.M. to get downtown to hers by six.

"Are you serious? He'll never be here then!" said True the night before, after Florrie told him her Sunday plans. She hadn't wanted to tell anyone, but she couldn't help it. "He'll be here at nine. No one could want to see a spirit that badly. Where do you find these people? But hey, I need you. Don't go. I will give you my Bear Beer bottle if you stay home tomorrow and do my English assignment," said True, waving some papers at her. Bear Beer was the first beer ever officially made in San Antonio. Florrie had been extremely irritated that True found that bottle at a neighbor's garage sale before she did.

She stared at him. She really wanted it.

"What about if I just help you with the paper when I get back? Or now?"

"Not enough."

"What is the topic?"

"Emerson."

"Emerson! Self-reliance! You think I can do your homework when it's about self-reliance? Forget that! The wolf-dog is waiting for me. I can hear him howling now."

"Snore. I can't believe the ways you fill your time."

They wandered, still jabbering, into the living room, where Ruben and Della were watching TV. "Shhh," said Della. "This is good. A psychiatrist is analyzing the nation." They both flopped down on the Oriental rug, True reaching for a couch pillow to stuff behind his head.

"It's a family moment!" said Ruben, grinning.

Ramsey arrived at 6:30 A.M, whistling. His bike had twenty-seven speeds. He refilled his water bottle from her hose. Florrie wore a gray bowling shirt with "Lupe" stitched over the pocket and gray cutoff jeans. No one in her family was up to meet him. Della reveled in late sleep on Sundays, her one day off.

Florrie loved to ride down the centers of old King William and Madison streets as fast as she could, fanning her arms out in the breeze. Cats darted back from the curb. A few sprinklers were hissing. You could own the streets that early. Even if festive public events had happened the night before, the streets bore only the softest echoes, and a few scattered plastic cups.

If it had been Saturday, Pablo, Florrie's neighbor two houses away, would be balancing tall ladders against the front of his blue and white house, building a new second-story porch. Pasquale de Leon would be wearing his blue overalls, arranging crates of fresh tomatoes and zucchini around his battered green truck in the parking lot down the street. He was the one who had caused Florrie to fall in love with turtles when she was a little girl. He would give her chunks of mango and papaya to pitch into the river and all the mysterious turtles would rise. If it were Saturday, Mr. Tiffin would be limping down the street carrying home three grapefruits and a small sack of snappy green beans. But Sunday was different. Not even the church bells were up yet.

Two dogs circled each other suspiciously in the

Keep San Antonio Beautiful Park. The autumn leaves were barely beginning to fall. Soon the sidewalks would be covered with crunchy pecans.

"I was thinking about you last night," Ramsey called back over his shoulder, pedaling ahead.

Florrie shivered. "Really? Why?"

"My parents had the new manager of Home Depot over for supper."

"You're joking."

"Also the manager of OfficeMax."

"You lie!" She was breathing normally again. "I hope you fed them tacks."

"They're on some city committee together."

"What, Keep San Antonio Ugly?"

"Be nice. I told them all about you."

"How could you? You barely know me!"

"No, I mean about your program thing. The anti-franchise deal."

"What did they say?"

"Nothing. They listened. My parents changed the subject, though."

"Lightfoot's Hardware closed!"

"Who?"

"Our neighborhood independent hardware shop. Thanks to Home Depot. Wish you had told them *that*."

"Do you think they would care?"

Florrie didn't answer.

Ramsey said, "Survival of the fittest and all."

"NO! Survival of the biggest! Lightfoot's was very fit. . . ."

He zoomed ahead of her, down Probandt, over the triple railroad tracks, bouncing with his hands out, past La Tuna bar surrounded by mounds of cacti, pecan trees, picnic tables, and an outdoor dance floor. "Hey, this place looks good! Do you go here?"

"Sometimes, for family parties . . . my dad goes there more. I mean, it's a *bar*."

"Is your dad the newspaper reporter? My dad said. Ruben Romo?"

Florrie said, "Yes!" She didn't want to talk about her dad. "Hey! I was reading a high school magazine from 1916 last night, really amazing ancient stuff, my neighbor Ingrid gave it to me, and it said . . ."

A noisy gravel truck passed them.

"It said—'GET A DANDY DRINK AT NESTER'S FOUNTAIN!'"

"WHERE IS NESTER'S FOUNTAIN?"

"Well, it used to be on San Pedro, near what used to be the San Pedro Springs Electric Park, you know about that? It was a soda fountain, but here's the cool thing—you can still see the lettering on the outside brick wall that says 'Nester . . .' and I never knew what it was before."

"Show it to me sometime."

His hair was flying backward. He had a wing on his head. She could feel the cave her heart lived in glowing as if an explorer had entered it with a torch.

They passed the ancient orphanage, a redbrick building set far back in a field. Ramsey slowed down to look at it. They passed the spot where the

Pig House used to be, now just an overgrown paved slab of concrete. Florrie pointed it out to Ramsey. "Do you know about the Pig House? I was partly responsible for getting it moved to downtown!"

They stopped and ate two potato-and-egg tacos each at Lucy's. As some of the first morning diners, they smiled at the few other diners conspiratorially. It gave you power to be up before everyone else. He said, "You look really good with hair that short. A lot of girls would not, but you do." He said, "My dad got food poisoning last week. From eating at some crummy fish franchise . . . thought you'd like that."

Florrie said, "Too bad!"

They passed the Mission Drive-In, one of the last outdoor theaters still operating in the United States, and Ramsey called out, "Do you ever go there?"

"Well sure, when we were little, with our parents. To see *Babe* and movies like that." She looked across at him hopefully. Maybe he would invite her to go there. Did he have a car?

At the San Jose Mission, they chained their bikes to a post and walked all around, past the Rose Window, through the arched rooms where priests used to live. Vines looped through open doorways. Volunteer palms poked up through cracks.

They stooped to peer into the little round ovens where the Indians used to bake their bread. They pointed out holes in the wall for gun barrels. They had mixed feelings about missions and missionaries. They sat in the shade of a live oak tree and discussed what a rotten deal Indians had gotten, all around.

When the visitors center opened, they watched the free movie about mission history in the cool viewing room. Florrie loved the singer Tish Hinojosa, who narrated the movie. Ramsey's hand crept gently into Florrie's lap and took her hand. She hadn't expected this so soon. Her heart pounded. She was sure he could feel it through her pulse. She looked over at him. He was staring straight ahead, at the Indians on the screen.

Down by Mission Espada, a few miles farther south, they remembered the wolf-dog, whom they'd pretty much forgotten about. They poked behind a bush, pretending to look for him. They lounged on a mown hillside to drink frosty lemonades they'd bought at a taco stand.

Ramsey said, "I kept thinking about you."

"You didn't."

He traced his finger along the line where her hair met her forehead. Florrie thought, *lips.* Her heart was thudding hard again. "I thought about you, too. I thought I dreamed it."

She looked off to the bright blue sky beyond the ancient stone mission chapel and took a deep breath. Cranes were flying overhead, elegant. *Lips.*

9 ~ survive

Florrie announced at dinner that evening that her family lived in a "vernacular Victorian" house. She was hoping no one would ask many details about her trip to the missions. The day felt delicate, precious, like newly classified information she would keep returning to when she was alone.

"What, did you crawl under it and find a tag?" said True.

"No. I went to a lecture on architecture a few days ago at the library. They showed slides."

"How fascinating."

* * *

Zip always declared that Florrie and True's house was his Refuge from Suburbia. He lived off Thousand Oaks, but called it Thousand Autos. Sometimes he showed up at their house unexpectedly. Florrie would find him rocking slowly in the yellow porch swing, watching the sky. Once she returned from the library and he was standing in her front yard wearing red suspenders, watering the Don Juan rosebush.

Lizzie said Florrie's house reminded her of a cottage that bears in the woods might live in, in a picture book. With its wraparound front porch, iron gate, two stocky palm trees in the front yard, and striped green awnings over the windows . . . Lizzie and Florrie had slept on the floor of the living room more than once, wrapped in quilts, watching old movies and eating popcorn.

Florrie tried to keep her room simple and neat as a monk's cell. She had an ancient white chenille bedspread that she'd bought from a garage sale, a burgundy Oriental rug on the wooden floor, and a

Moroccan hassock. She had a stumpy white candle in a tin cup on her desk and a small, chipped, blue-painted pitcher from Italy.

Florrie collected old postcards. The messages, sent from people she had not known to people she would never know, were haunting and abrupt. "Arrived safely" or "Paul is better." One card said simply, "We think the baby will survive," with no further details. Florrie kept the postcards tied in thick stacks with red satin ribbons, in two large baskets next to her desk. There was something deeply comforting about their thick stock and calm, rectangular shapes.

Florrie usually bought her cards at junk and thrift stores, but Mr. Tiffin had given her a fat stack of images when the Hertzberg Circus Museum closed down: the lady with glossy hair to the floor, Tom Thumb in his glittering carriage, with his teeny-tiny violin, and the "world's largest miniature circus"—intricate tents, trapezes, elephants, and clowns.

"They're seconds," Tiffin had said about the cards. He had been curator, ticket taker, and duster of odd artifacts at the Hertzberg for years. "They were in a box all tucked away in a back closet. Copies. Never on display. We have loads of them. I know it's a little illicit, but I thought they'd be much happier with you."

Once, at a yard sale down the street, Florrie had found a large bundle of cards tied with thin pink ribbon (three dollars) perched on a table between a white ceramic cream pitcher shaped like a cow (five dollars) and an old lady's gigantic silken bra (six dollars). She had counted out three ones while trying not to act too excited.

Florrie's favorite postcards stood against the lamp on her desk. The ostrich race at Hot Wells. A train wreck in graphic black and white with three words on back: "No one hurt." She gazed at them while struggling with Algebra Two, fingering them as if they could carry her dreams into their lost, hand-tinted worlds. She wanted to *go there*. And she could not.

Lizzie, who decorated her own room by pinning up favorite prom pictures and singers, as well as movie ticket stubs and take-out menus, found Florrie's pale gray walls, without a single bulletin board or poster, odd. But Beth didn't. Beth said, "Watch the shadows. She has the most active walls of any of us."

Florrie liked empty spaces to rest her eyes on. She liked the softness cast by a low lamp burning at her bedside in the evenings. She was working on a theory that everything on earth depended on *lighting*.

That was the problem. The modern world was a *glare*. Florrie's notebook on her desk was open to a page that said: "Gap. Used to be just normal GapClothes, but GapEverything now. GapBaby, GapBathtub, GapHouse, GapBrain."

The campaign was definitely gaining power as it went along. Ruben rediscovered a favorite haunt of his youth, Tucker's Café, soul food and soul music, over on the east side, and was touched when an elderly waitress remembered him. Why had he ever stopped going there?

Della and True bought new walking and running shoes at a tiny store over on West Avenue instead of at Dillard's. They stopped at Lucy's Bakery next door to the shoe shop, in a 1950s strip mall, and brought home a box of *pan dulce*, which they placed on a china pedestal at the center of the dining table. Ruben sat on the couch at midnight watching the Weather Channel, picking sweet crumbs off his sweater.

Zip said he was renting a permanent table at Earl Abel's Restaurant. He loved their fried chicken and mashed potatoes and the waitress who called him Baby Doll. Lizzie reported she'd gotten her mom to stop at a neighborhood shoe repair shop that they'd never even noticed before and they fixed her favorite broken purse for *two dollars*.

"And listen what happened with my dad, man."

Juan was enthusiastically promoting the project with his parents, whom he described as "the city's greatest consumers."

"I was begging my dad, support the little guys, and he stopped at this farmer's market on Jackson-Keller and found his long-lost cousin, man, this dude he's been looking for, like, twenty years? Who disappeared from us because he was an alcoholic and really messed up, and now he's not only straight, he's a farmer!"

Bailey said he had discovered a couple of great small cafés, Vietnamese and Indian, close to his house that he had never taken the time to enter before. He also walked into two other stores, one for T-shirts and one for electronics, asked, "Is this store part of a chain?" then turned on his heel and left when they said, "Yes."

"You should tell them why you're leaving," Florrie reminded him. "We can spread the word in more ways than one."

* * *

A reporter from the *Current* called Florrie and asked her some questions, then wrote a very positive story in *Boldface* and placed it in *a box*. To Florrie's pleasure and surprise, it was a call to action for other citizens. The page was topped by a huge, terrific cartoon—chain-store facsimiles with slashes across them and a group of cool-looking teens with crossed arms standing firmly, determinedly, in the foreground. They wore aprons that said, "Buy Independent!!!"

And then two other television stations called her. The reporters came over to her house on the same afternoon and interviewed her under the giant pecan trees when no one else was home. "How many people are part of your campaign?" asked one.

Florrie answered, "Friends, classmates, family, neighbors—more than I can count."

10 ～ onward

Two weeks later Florrie invited the members of the campaign over to her house to see how everyone was doing and to plot their next moves. Florrie said a dramatic public statement was in order, so they had decided to drape the Wal-Mart sign on Jones-Maltsberger Road with big white sheets.

Juan arrived before the others, wearing a small brown suede Stetson, like the hats old men wear.

"You look good, Juan," said Florrie. His long black hair curled out from under the hat.

"I *am* good. Can I fan through your postcards? I'll be careful, promise."

Like Florrie, Juan felt intrigued by the ancient

postmarks, one-cent stamps, men with ponytails and chiseled profiles, and the spectacular penmanship of the messages. Were all those correspondents dead now? They must be dead.

Zip appeared, seeming rather grumpy, saying he was starving, asking for enchiladas. Lizzie brought a green-tea bottle filled with two tall stalks of fragrant tuberoses—not the easiest thing to carry across town. Bailey carried an article from an out-of-town paper about a woman fighting superstores in Illinois.

Ramsey showed up late, wearing an Alamo Heights Swim Team T-shirt. Zip stared hard at Florrie as she introduced Ramsey around the circle of Keystone students, beaming.

"Did you take up swimming, Florrie?" he asked her.

"No, I picked her up on the River Walk," Ramsey said. "She was fishing."

"I was not!"

Ramsey ran his hand across Florrie's cheek and gently pinched the bottom of her earlobe. Then he flopped down on the couch next to Juan, rubbed his hands together, and said, "Is anyone else coming?" Then, "Plans of action, shoot!"

They had been talking about their Wal-Mart Sign Draping Project for days now and needed to make firm plans. They would do it next Saturday, since they were not in school and it was the store's biggest shopping day. "What about security guards?" Ramsey asked.

"Do they *have* one?" Florrie asked. "All night?"

Ramsey thought everyone had one by now. They had video cameras, too. Maybe not on the *sign*, but on the store. Someone should make a test run before the draping to see if there was a guard pacing out front. Hopefully he was inside, asleep at a little table. "Okay, that's your job," said Juan to Ramsey. "Check it out. Let us know."

Lizzie thought they should drape more than one sign on the same morning (she despised the Lowe's superstore on I-10 that had just cut down an ancient oak tree despite objections from local tree preservationists), but Florrie thought two signs was one more than they could handle. "There's the crane to consider," she said. "I think I can only talk Mando into doing this once. If the signs were on ground level, it would be a different story."

Ramsey hopped up and said, "You know what? I'll need to check my swimming schedule. I think we might be going to Laredo next weekend. So what about in two weeks?" He grabbed a handful of tortilla chips from the bowl on a side table.

"Two weeks from now is better for me, too," said Zip. "I have *so much* science fair work and also a hot date."

Everyone stared at him.

"With a model from Tuscaloosa."

Florrie tipped her head. Was he joking?

"What can I say? She *heard* of me," Zip said, shrugging. "From my cousin who knows her. She sent me an e-mail wanting to get together when she comes to San Antonio for that beauty pageant next week. Little Miss Teenie Bean or something. Asked if I'd wander the River Walk with her. Show her stuff."

"*You* with a beauty contestant?" Bailey roared, rolling backward on the floor. "This I must see!"

"I have inner beauty, my friends."

"Will we be contacting the media in advance?" Lizzie asked.

"For Zip's date?" Bailey couldn't stop laughing.

Florrie looked from Zip to Bailey and back at Zip. "Let the media find us. If they want to. We can't make it feel too—calculated—though it *is* planned. It *has* to be planned."

Ramsey checked his watch for the tenth time. "Going, guys. Nice to meet you all. Hail to the chief!" He kissed Florrie on the cheek. "And *you*"—he pointed at Zip—"take it easy."

11 ~ geronimo

Days went by, notes on a musical score.

Florrie and Ramsey talked on the phone almost every evening. Sometimes he called; sometimes she did.

"How did you get so obsessed with all this?" he asked her one night as they wandered along the river after her restaurant shift ended at nine. He liked the restaurant. He had been very complimentary to her mother, though he didn't eat anything. He said it looked "authentic."

Florrie told him about her trip to Mobile, Alabama, with her father when she was a little girl, how they ate grits and scrambled eggs in a tiny café called the Little Kitchen, so small it didn't have a sign outdoors; they had to ask its name. Her father said, "Take a good look. Soon you won't see places like this anymore," and Florrie started crying.

She told him how she and her dad had helped to get the Pig House, San Antonio's first drive-in restaurant, moved from the south side to the parking lot at the Pig Stand Restaurant on South St. Mary's.

She told him how her grandpa from Lebanon, Hani Hamza, used to walk with her and her brother all over downtown and point out the places where great lost things used to be. Frost Brothers. Joske's department store. Quinney's Just Good Food. She could say their names even if she had never seen them.

Ramsey had a kind way of listening and of making her feel more interesting than she believed she was. He kissed the inside of her wrist. He laughed hard at things she said: for example, when she somberly described her aversion to instant messaging. She said it "sucked her brains out." He kept placing his hands around her head all afternoon, saying, "Stay, brains, stay."

One afternoon Ramsey came downtown and they rode the open-air trolley together in a big circle, past the hospitals and the Mercado, the giant red "Torch of Friendship" and Alamo Plaza, standing up in the space like a balcony at the back, waving at pedestrians at crosswalks. They rode twice around downtown without getting off.

Ramsey looked at the city half the time and the other half he looked at Florrie. He matched his hand to hers, slowly turning her silver bracelet back over when it flipped upside down on her arm. He stared at her without blinking. Holding his eyes quite firmly on her face as she spoke, which her parents and brother never did. Which few people did, if you thought about it. There was magnetism in such a gaze.

They rode the elevator to the top of the Tower of the Americas at sundown. The sky layered soft purple to the west, shot through with a brilliant pink line. The city glittered in all directions. Ramsey stood behind Florrie and put his arms around her and his chin on her shoulder. "Umm," he said. "You always smell so good. What is that?"

"Sandalwood."

He looked out to the far hills over her shoulder and said, "Let's drive to Bandera."

She giggled. "Let's drive south to George West!"

Another afternoon, after Ramsey's swim practice, they rode their bikes from the two directions of their houses to meet at old Fort Sam Houston, a military base. The Quadrangle grounds were a wide, grassy, central meadow hemmed in by hundred-year-old stone buildings—free for roaming or picnicking and better than a park. Tame deer, rabbits, peacock, and quail wandered around confidently, and visitors could walk and sit among them.

Long ago an army general who loved animals had brought some wounded deer to the compound to heal. He grew fond of having animals right outside his door, so the tradition continued. Also, the Apache chief Geronimo and members of his tribe had once been held as captives in the same compound. Florrie knew this; Ramsey didn't. He found it hard to believe. There was actually a post-card photograph made of Geronimo there, which Ingrid kept in her collection.

Florrie carried apples in her backpack.

A young speckled deer approached Florrie and Ramsey where they sprawled on the grass. It munched one of Florrie's tiny Gala apples thoughtfully, then began licking Ramsey's head. "Yecccchhhhh," he said, reaching up to find his hair all wet on one side. "Deer saliva!"

He pushed the deer away. But it kept coming back.

"Oh, I love this natural habitat," Ramsey said, lying back on his wadded-up blue-jean jacket. "Deer tongues and all. Maybe they'll hold us captive here after we drape the Wal-Mart sign."

An enormous brown rabbit curled at Florrie's side. She placed her hand on its plump belly and held it there gently, not stroking, just feeling the quiet heartbeat inside and the warm fur. It was amazing to be able to touch a rabbit you didn't really know. The rabbit looked only a tiny bit concerned, then closed its eyes again.

12 ~ stand up and be counted

Florrie and her committee created enormous banners out of white thrift-store bedsheets. They painted the giant words with blazing blood-red paint Florrie found among the clutter of paint cans in her family's back shed. Why did her family own any paint that color?

Wal-Mart advertised "We Sell For Less" on all its signs. Florrie painted:

LESS IMAGINATION
LESS INDEPENDENCE
LESS CREATIVITY

Bailey and Juan painted:

LESS INDIVIDUALISM
LESS LITTLE BUSINESSES
LESS LOVELY TOWNS

They discussed whether to use "cities" or "towns" and chose "towns." Actually, that was a lot of words to paint on bedsheets. They took great pains to be neat.

Then they laid the sheets out all over the grass in Florrie's backyard to dry.

Florrie went inside and got lemonade for everybody. Zip sprawled on his back on the ground. Lizzie talked to the ducks over the fence. Juan and Bailey discussed the Unlimited Thought Bookstore, where they had recently attended a discussion on Cosmic Unpredictability.

"Where's Ramsey?" Zip asked. His eyes were closed.

"He had to swim. And Beth had to go see her grandma in the hospital."

Using a giant needle Florrie found in her own grandmother's wooden sewing box, they connected the sheets along the top edge with heavy-duty twine, leaving a well-discussed space between them, with the twine looped out as a large, loose seam. The hardest part was pulling it through. They could fling the sheets over the sign like a tent and their own words would hang down below "We Sell For Less." It would be perfect.

The next day Florrie packed her overnight bag and went to spend the night at Lizzie's, because Lizzie lived on the north side of town, very close to Wal-Mart. To sneak out of Florrie's own house in the middle of the night would have been difficult, since her father was often awake at odd hours, reading on the couch.

Lizzie, wrapped in a pink quilt, groaned when Florrie rose at 2 A.M. Only two people could fit in the crane. But they were all going to be there, perched somewhere in the shadows, for moral support.

"I *hate* waking up," said Lizzie. She covered her face with the pillow.

"So does Zip," Florrie said, punching Lizzie's cell phone at her and tugging the pillow off. "At least he says he does. Call him. I'm getting dressed. He was going to keep his cell in his bed because his alarm hasn't been working, and he has to pick everyone up because Juan's car is broken. But hurry because I have to call Mando, too. *He's* the most crucial one!"

Ramsey was outside idling at the curb in his mother's blue Maxima. They tiptoed out Lizzie's front door, hoping her dachshund, Ace (probably sleeping with her parents), wouldn't wake up and bark.

With some difficulty, Florrie had talked her cousin Mando, a twenty-seven-year-old professional tree trimmer, into meeting them in his yellow truck equipped with a full-scale crane—he was not *at all* excited about getting out of bed at such an hour, not to mention doing something illicit in the dark. A week before, Florrie had sneaked him a rather large gift certificate (she would pay for it from her own earnings later) to El Viento to convince him to do this. He was a big fan of the restaurant's special super-chalupas. "Pleeeeze, Mando! Remember when you used to come in and I would always bring you extra *beans*?!"

"Aw man, Florrie, beans are hardly a trade for a *crane*."

To encourage him, she also invoked their grandfather, whom he had adored. "Hani would be so proud of you, come on!"

When he was a teenager, Mando had once felt sorry for the monkey in the cage at the West Side Feed Store and let him out. The monkey, who scooted through the open side door of the shop before anyone noticed he was loose (with Mando hot on his heels), stayed missing for three days. He was finally discovered soaking in Lupe Pacheco's birdbath and returned to captivity. Mando hadn't done anything creative like that in quite a while.

"You're getting old, man! Where is your verve?" Florrie had asked.

"Okay, girl," Mando said, "you got me. But I *shop* at those big stores. What if they ban me or something?"

Ramsey parked his car a block away from the Wal-Mart lot. They sat inside for a minute, looking around at the quiet street. A street lamp cast a pool of yellow light onto the pavement. The parking lot's lights were dimmed since the store was closed. Ramsey spoke softly. "Did you know the Wal-Mart on Loop 1604 is open twenty-four hours? We could not do this there."

They stepped out into the chilly morning air and started walking, gingerly, up the block. Florrie whispered, "It's amazing how you can feel a little guilty even when you're doing what you believe in." Then Zip and his groggy passengers rolled up and pulled sideways into a driveway across the road and parked between some crepe myrtle bushes.

Mando drove into the lot shortly afterward. Florrie noticed that his yellow truck made a rattling sound. He backed the truck right under the sign and turned it off. There were no cars in the store's parking lot, except one right up near the building, which Florrie imagined belonged to the mysterious watchman.

Bailey, Zip, and Juan were climbing out of Zip's car, stretching and speaking in low voices. Zip popped his trunk open and took out the folded sheets. Florrie ran to her friends across the dark street from her cousin's truck. "After you hand us the sheets, maybe you should come back over here into the shadows," she whispered. "So you don't attract attention from passing cars or anything."

Zip whispered back, "Don't you think a passerby at this hour would have other things to think about? Like, dreamland?"

"She's right," Lizzie said. "The crane could be a store crane, for all anybody knows. Like one of those changing-the-signs cranes . . . But if we're all mobbed around and someone sees us, it might look suspicious."

"I want to be there if Florrie falls out, to catch her!" said Juan.

"I wish you hadn't said that," whispered Florrie. "But I think Lizzie's right. You should watch from across the street."

Still, they accompanied her toward Mando's truck for a send-off. Lizzie and Bailey actually tiptoed. Ramsey was already climbing into the bucket. He had told Florrie he was not scared of heights at all. That's why he could do high dives.

Florrie climbed in, too, with Ramsey offering a steadying handhold and Zip giving her a gentle boost. Then Zip handed over the sheets. "Okay, pals, we're heading back for the shadows now," he said. "Good luck! Don't fall out!"

Florrie found it creepy going up in the bucket. It reminded her of a Ferris wheel, which she hated. Her stomach lurched and wavered. She steadied her eyes on the sign and gripped the side. The sky felt dark and distant. Ramsey was chattering in a low voice, "Little more, little higher, almost there . . ." as Mando monitored the lever that raised the crane. "Oh God, I feel dizzy," Florrie said. She closed her eyes.

When she cracked them open, the crane was at the same height as the sign. A little wind had kicked up. Was it windier because they were at a slightly higher altitude?

Florrie looked over the edge. "Ye-ow!"

Ramsey said, "Easy, baby, don't look down. Just look straight ahead."

Florrie unfolded the sheets carefully and handed Ramsey his corners.

Together they leaned out over the side. The bucket tipped a little and Florrie said, "Aye-yi-yi!"

Ramsey said, "Ready?"

Florrie counted off, "One, two, three," then they both flung the backside sheet over the top of the sign. It slid down into place, with the seam at the sign's upper edge. The width of the sheets was perfect. Florrie leaned out, patting the sheet on their sides, making sure everything was hanging straight.

Then Mando lowered the crane a bit and drove slowly around to the other side so they could smooth those sheets, too. "We calculated very accurately!" Florrie laughed. Their painted words hung right below "We Sell For Less."

Ramsey, laughing, tried to kiss Florrie before the bucket was lowered, but she felt too dizzy to kiss. "I will never be a tree trimmer," she said, brushing Ramsey's cheek with her lips and holding them there a moment.

When they were done and the crane was being lowered, it made a loud squeaking noise. Florrie said, "Omigod, I hope that night watchman's asleep!"

Ramsey said, "No sign of him. He's sacked out!"

Down on earth again, Florrie leaned in Mando's window and kissed him on the cheek, too. "Thank you, my favorite cousin!" she said. "You're a hero, Mando!"

"Yeah, baby, but I'm feeling like a criminal—so lemme outta here."

"Keep your lights off till you get out of the parking lot!" Florrie said.

Mando sped away and Florrie and Ramsey stood back to look at the sheets. Now she could laugh. "It looks incredible!"

"Very professional," said Ramsey.

"The width is perfect!" said Florrie. "Good thing the sheets were king-size!"

Florrie and Ramsey dashed across the street to confer with the others. It was now 3:42 A.M. They could hear their friends clapping in the car.

"Very cool," said Zip, hanging out the window. "It looks great and kind of surreal. Look how they're rippling just a tiny bit in the breeze. Good job, guys! Florrie, we *hated* staying in the car; we wanted to be cheering in the parking lot!"

Florrie said, "I could feel you."

Zip said, "I didn't do any work this morning, but I'm starving. Are you guys hungry? How weird is it to eat before four A.M.?"

"Is Taqueria No Que No open?" asked Bailey.

"At this hour? Are you crazy?" said Juan. "The only things open are Mi Tierra and the police station."

"I'm cold," said Lizzie.

Florrie shivered, wrapped her jacket tighter, leaned into their window, and said, "I'd sort of like to stay here till the store opens. Just be invisible and watch what people do. When they see it."

Lizzie said, "Are you crazy? That's many hours from now. And they'll get you."

A low-rider roared past very fast in the lane closest to them, pumping out a throb of bass. Florrie and Ramsey pressed against the car. "I don't want to get killed next to Wal-Mart," Florrie said.

"I don't want to get killed anywhere," Ramsey said, grabbing her hand. "Mi Tierra!" he said. "Okay, meet you guys there!" They hopped into the car and headed back downtown on San Pedro. Mi Tierra had odd diners at that early hour. A large table of bald boxers with towels over their giant shoulders ("So *that's* who uses the twenty-four-hour gym," whispered Bailey), a few mariachis with silver spangles up and down their legs, and some tourists who probably had jetlag, speaking in German.

"I am going to order a very large fruit bowl," announced Ramsey. "Which I have never eaten here before. Has anyone had it? Is it good?"

"I am going to order the largest *huevos rancheros* platter there is," said Zip, with a hand on his forehead.

The waiter in a white jacket gave them very good service. He didn't seem sleepy at all.

They toasted one another with their water glasses and ate happily and slowly. The boxers in towels rose and left.

"I keep thinking about the sheets flapping as the workers drive into the parking lot," said Bailey.

"Like flags of surrender. Our culture has surrendered."

"It is not the workers' fault," said Juan. "They just need jobs, man."

"Of course they do," said Bailey. "We all do."

"I have a job," said Florrie. "I mean, the restaurant. Anyone want to help me?"

"I cut yards, period," said Zip. "In the summer. I talk to the little grasses and they say, 'Good-bye! Good-bye!'"

Ramsey grinned. "I don't have time for a job. Swim practice takes all my time." He looked at his watch. "Omigod, good thing I mentioned it! Gotta go, guys! Why don't you watch the morning news and see if any waving sheets are on it?"

They rose and paid their bill to the extremely groggy cashier at the counter. Lizzie wandered over into the doorway of the darkened bar, where a TV was always playing. "The news is on!" she said. "Let's watch the news just in case the sheets are on it!"

But it was all about a chemical spill from a train

south of town and sad car wrecks in the night.

"They don't know about it yet," said Lizzie.

"But are we so sure it would even *be* on the news?" asked Bailey. "Like, every new wall of graffiti that goes up in the night doesn't make it onto the news."

Florrie glared at him. "This is not graffiti."

"To them it will be," he said.

Lizzie, Juan, and Bailey thought they'd better get home or their parents might find them gone and think they'd eloped. "What, with one another?" Zip said. "Okay, I'll drive you." Florrie's family would think she was still at Lizzie's.

They drove through the tranquil Saturday morning streets—past the Blanco Café and Taqueria No Que No and Chris Madrid's. They also drove past Super Target and CompUSA and Office Depot. One by one Lizzie, Bailey, and Juan stepped out, with Florrie hopping from the car each time to hug them good-bye and thank them.

Zip and Florrie remained. Florrie climbed into

the front seat next to him. "And you, my dear?" said Zip. "A little car service toward downtown now for you? Wait a minute, how come you're still here? We were near *your* house when we were at Mi Tierra!"

"I know," Florrie said softly. "But I want to go back to Wal-Mart."

"What?" said Zip. "Words I never thought I'd hear you say!"

"I want to see what's going on over there. I'm not satisfied just leaving."

"What if they catch you?"

"Us," said Florrie. "You, too."

"Great. What if they catch *us?*"

She shrugged. "They won't."

They pulled up onto the edge of the parking lot, across the street from where Zip had parked earlier. Florrie laughed. "In the dark we couldn't see how truly *great* the sheets looked," she said. "Am I just imagining it, or is everybody really slowing down?"

A few cars on Jones-Maltsberger Road passed, drivers and passengers peering from windows to take in the gently billowing sheets hanging from the sign. The words gleamed electric red in the early morning light.

They sat in the car and watched.

A man and a woman in floral hats walked past them with a waddling beagle on a leash. They seemed to pause, look at the sheets, and say something to each other. Zip said, "Florrie, actually this campaign is more fun than I imagined it would be in the beginning. Even if I *am* really hungry for a Waffle House breakfast—"

Florrie interrupted. "Why don't you just buy a waffle iron and cook some skinny, crispy little waffles for yourself?"

"Not the same. Seriously, I do feel somewhat changed. Mostly in the way I think."

Florrie said, "I love you."

"You do not," said Zip, "You only like me for my car. I was thinking I might write a letter to the

Austin American Statesman and make *you* sign it. Your dad doesn't work for *that* paper."

Florrie said, "What about?"

"People in Austin are now wearing buttons that say 'Keep Austin Weird'—isn't that sort of like what we're doing? We could salute them?"

Florrie said, "Hmm, that's very cool. I hadn't heard about it. What kind of weirdness are they referring to?"

"I think our kind. Independence and stuff."

Florrie said, "Do we need buttons, too? What would they say? Wait! Look, are people gathering in a little clump over there by the sign? I think so! God, people like to shop a lot! Look how many cars pulled in since we got here! And it's still early. Aren't those other people moving toward the sheets? We have to get out! Let's go see what they're doing!"

They walked over to the rim of the crowd. The bright white concrete of the parking lot had been mended with black tar along some cracks. The squiggly lines looked like a secret map. Shiny silver carts clattering bumpily toward vehicles, pushed by grumpy-looking early birds, were stuffed with bulky white sacks. Shop, shop, shop. Zip actually helped an elderly man unload something large, like a hose system. Two boys with uncombed blond hair badgered their mother for M&M's. She didn't want to get them out of the bag. The mother was staring at an elderly woman in a bright purple jumpsuit who pointed at the softly fluttering sheets as if they were hers, and spoke in a high-pitched voice. "This used to be a beautiful field! I used to walk my dog in it! We were doing just fine in those days! My shoe store closed because of this place!"

A couple of middle-aged ladies nodded their heads. There were about eight older people in the circle. Florrie thought, *No teenagers shop this early in the day.*

Mr. Van Winkle, the store manager (according to his name tag), walked up from behind the corral for carts, passed directly in front of Florrie, and stared perplexedly at the lady in purple. He had a stunned, intensely florid look on his face. "Ma'am, what's the commotion? You are welcome to walk your dog in this parking lot or on the moon, for all I care. Please move along! And are you responsible for this mess?" He waved at the sheets.

The woman said, "You can't tell me to move along. It's a free country."

"It's a less free country, thanks to you!" another woman, in an orange Don't Mess With Texas sweatshirt, said. "Look at those signs! They're right! But here we are, making the most of it!"

Mr. Van Winkle sighed. "You are creating a disturbance," he said to both of them. "What is your problem?"

He walked a few paces away from where Florrie stood, turned his back on them, and made a call on his cell phone.

Only two minutes later, it seemed, a police car pulled into the lot. A tall young policeman with a red crew cut stepped out and Mr. Van Winkle went over to talk to him. They were both staring up at the sheets as Mr. Van Winkle gestured, looking irritated. The policeman walked over to the crowd of people.

He pointed at the sign. "Is the person responsible for—this—here?" He paused a minute between words, as if he didn't know what to call the sheets.

Florrie gulped.

The woman in the purple jumpsuit said, "The sign is true! What it says."

"But did you do that?" The policeman looked up at the sheets and back at the woman, as if he couldn't imagine how she *could* do that, even if she wanted to. He grinned. "Where's your ladder?"

The woman paused, looking defiant. Now Florrie gasped. Was she going to take credit for it?

The woman said, "In my back pocket!"

Zip leaned over Florrie and whispered, "This is a little nuts."

The policeman motioned to the group with his arm and pointed to the sheets with his other hand. "Anybody here know about this?"

There was a pause the size of a red car passing.

"I did it!" Florrie blurted.

The manager, who had not even looked in her direction before, turned, startled. "Ma'am?"

It was the first time anyone had ever called Florrie "ma'am." She didn't like it.

"I mean, *we*," she said. "We did it. We didn't get any paint on your sign."

The policeman looked her up and down with vague interest. "Who is *we?*" he asked.

And now Florrie remembered something. Something she'd learned in her quick research about trespassing and property, and she stepped back onto the public sidewalk, grabbing Zip by the hand and pulling him back with her, off the Wal-Mart parking lot pavement, just a few steps.

"*We*," Florrie declared, "are the people who like little stores, not big stores, and hate what's happening to our cities and towns. Big chains come in like vacuums and everything else disappears!"

No one said anything, so she just continued.

"*We*," Florrie said, "like decent architecture, too. Does this look like architecture to you?" She waved her hand at the flat-faced store. Heads in the crowd turned and stared at the store as if they had not seen it before.

"Hell no!" a man with no hair shouted.

Florrie said, "Has anyone heard what happened in Floresville right down the road when a superstore opened and the drugstore that was there for fifty years had to shut down, because they were undercutting their prices, and then after it shut down, the superstore raised the prices?"

Now a larger crowd had gathered. Florrie said, "It's not the only place that happened, either."

A very tubby man with a cart stared at Florrie openmouthed. The policeman seemed to be speaking to someone on a walkie-talkie. Was he calling in extra forces?

"She's a nut!" Mr. Van Winkle said.

"It's a free country!" insisted the woman in purple. Another husky shopper in a camouflage jacket who looked as if he ate deer jerky for breakfast said, "So go somewhere else if you don't like it!"

Florrie retorted, "But somewhere else is disappearing!"

Zip spoke for the first time. "I'd rather use less and pay more!" he said.

The policeman pointed at Zip. "Are you part of *we*?"

"*Oui, oui!*" said Zip, who was the only one of Florrie's friends taking French instead of Spanish. He waved his hand in the air, palm up, as a flourish.

The policeman laughed.

Mr. Van Winkle said, "I'd like them to get off my property."

The policeman said to Florrie and Zip, "I suggest you leave these premises and don't return. If you do, the manager can call us to have you arrested for trespassing."

Florrie pointed down at their feet, so he'd notice they were not on the parking lot at that moment. "Don't worry," she said. "We won't come back." To Mr. Van Winkle she said, "I wouldn't shop here if this were the only store in town. Which is what it wants to be!"

He said nothing but turned away from her and began walking toward the store.

Florrie put out her hand to shake the policeman's hand. Would he order them to take down the sheets? He did not. She would keep thinking about that in days to come. He shook her hand right back, grinned with half his mouth, pointed at the sheets, and said, "You must have a *heck* of a ladder."

Before Florrie and Zip could cross the street back to Zip's car, a little green pickup truck slowed next to them, and the reporter from the newspaper who'd written the story about her before leaned out and said, "Florrie!"

It took her a second to recognize him. She had written him a thank-you letter after his nice coverage. "I was listening to the police radio and wasn't far away . . ." he said, "and I noticed"—he pointed at the sheets and the crowd—"and wondered, could it be? And here you are!" He pulled out a notepad. "Do you have time for a few remarks? I've got my camera, too!"

The next day the story miraculously appeared in the center of Sunday's front page (Florrie had figured back page, metro section—maybe?) with a clear color photograph of the banners, a large headline, TEENS OUTRAGED BY LOSS OF INDEPENDENT BUSINESSES, and Florrie and Zip standing in front of them grinning.

Florrie's hair looked electric.

13 ~ dubious

"I can't believe your publicity quotient," True said on Monday evening, standing in the doorway of Florrie's bedroom, munching tortilla chips. For once neither of them had to work. Their mother was trying out a new busboy who'd just moved to the city from Cotulla, Texas. Florrie thought they should write him a thank-you letter too. "Pretty amazing news coverage. Obviously there wasn't much going on in the world. I can't *believe* Mando helped you out. Good thing you didn't put his name in the paper; he would have killed you."

She didn't say anything so he went on. "Dad was *shocked*. Could you believe his face? He seemed to mellow out, though. I do think you think too much. Say, are you a Mennonite now?"

Florrie was wearing a baggy gray shirt and some gray cotton pants, with pale gray socks. True dropped a chip on the floor. She turned her head to say, "Hello! Pick it up!"

"You should just let your mind—sail—with the seasons, Florrie. Don't you ever relax?"

"I thought I was sprawled on my bed right now; doesn't it look that way to you?"

Her chenille spread was folded neatly at her feet. A silver bowl of popcorn sat beside her. She was taking a break from her oral history project, reading *A Sand County Almanac* by Aldo Leopold, published in 1949. Eliza Gilkyson was singing from her new CD. Florrie was a specialist at giving herself delicious study breaks. And she'd been working for *hours*.

Florrie felt so relieved that her English teacher had substituted a family history paper for the traditional research term paper. If your person was deceased, you used your own memory and interviewed people who had known him.

Florrie had stopped by Mr. Pencil to copy Grandpa Hani's immigration documents, which were half in English and half in Arabic, and was going to use them for a cover sheet. She still couldn't believe True had written *his* paper the year before about Grandpa Julio, Ruben's father, who died before they were born. She picked up her legal pad from beside her bed and waved it at her brother. "True, leave me alone; I'm working on my research paper," Florrie said. "So tell me again, why did you write about Grandpa Julio instead of Hani?"

"Because if I wrote about Hani—you dimwit— I would have too much to say."

"You're lying. You didn't write about Hani because it would make you too sad."

True didn't answer.

He wore a black leather jacket over a black T-shirt, with streaky bleached blue jeans and cowboy boots. Florrie figured he must be going out with his friends and was just taking a moment to torment her first.

He didn't answer, so Florrie asked, "What is your problem?"

"Me? I have no problem! I am—*peaceful*. But you're . . . a walking, talking problem. Always worrying, always turning everything over and over in your brain—don't you get tired of it? I get tired just living in the same house with you. This is supposed to be a fun time in our lives!"

She swung her legs over and sat up. "Sigh."

He cocked his head. "I think wearing only one color seems more like something a franchise lover would do." She stared at him.

Then he said, "Did you ever think how franchises that come into a neighborhood essentially complement that neighborhood? They say, 'We notice there are people here, who might need to *eat* or *shop*.' They recognize humanity! I haven't gone into one in, like, a hundred years, thanks to your bossiness, but I do seem to remember that."

"No, they prey upon humanity," Florrie said. "They say, 'We see you; we will get your money.' Today it's so unbelievable, the business section of the newspaper said Wal-Mart is threatening both Toys 'R' Us and Blockbuster. I mean, I realize they're *all* franchises, but don't you think that's ironic?"

"You read the *business* section?" True asked. "I can't believe it. Boring! Anyhow, if they're all threatening one another, maybe they'll spontaneously combust."

She sighed. "Centuries ago the Mongols were fighting the Muslims and now, True is bugging Florrie."

"Florrie, I hate to tell you this, but I need new contact lenses and I am going to get them at Wal-Mart. The price difference between there and that rinky-dink optical joint is huge. But I've been a good boy like the rest of you nutcases so you can grant me one little exception, okay?"

He had wandered over to her desk and picked up her half-finished letter to the editor. She always hand-wrote her letters before typing them on the computer.

"Who'll sign it this time?"

"I'm going to ask Zip."

"Didn't he sign the one last month? I couldn't *believe* his real name is Frederick!"

"Yeah, but he liked it. He got a lot of compliments. Or Ramsey, maybe."

"Not Ramsey."

"Why not?"

"I don't know." True looked at her. "Don't you think there's something—*about*—that guy?"

"What do you mean?"

"He seems very—conscious of how he seems."

"Huh?"

"A little slick."

"Slick?" said Florrie. Her brother in a black leather jacket was calling someone else slick?

"Like he's looking in a mirror—when there isn't a mirror."

Florrie shook her head. True didn't usually act this zen strange.

"That's ridiculous," she said. "You don't even know him." She changed the subject. "Do you think that's a good letter?"

If you drove north on San Pedro, mammoth poles holding enormous signs poked their heads up everywhere—Radio Shack, Big Lots, Walgreens. The poles had been getting bigger and bigger. Often the signs were shiny yellow or orange, cluttering the sky.

Florrie's letter said this new trend toward larger and taller monster signs should be outlawed as visual pollution. If people needed to find a business, they could learn to find it without all that fanfare. Everyone should join Scenic Texas, which was anti-billboard and pro-tree.

"Go to Vermont," True mumbled, stuffing a large handful of her popcorn into his mouth. "If I recall, the signs in Vermont are two inches tall."

"Truly?"

"Yeah, it's official up there. Remember I told you how hard it was to find anything because the signs were so small? I think they don't have any Wal-Marts, either. Maybe it's your future home."

"Why are they so smart and we're so dumb?"

"And they like old houses more than new ones and everybody has pots of geraniums on their porches and lace curtains and *incredibly* obese felines and you could wear a long gray pioneer skirt and bake snickerdoodles. . . . I don't know if they'd like your haircut, though."

True had gone to camp in Vermont one summer and held it under her nose that he'd now seen the north, which she hadn't. He didn't even *like* the camp. Everybody stayed in their bunks reading books half the day. For this he traveled across the country?

"I think you are secretly on my team."

True snorted, turning on his heel. "Team! Why didn't you just play soccer or basketball if you were desperate for a team? Oh well, it's your distinguishing characteristic. If you vanished, I'd have to put that on your Wanted poster: 'Distinguishing characteristic: obsessed with the past.'"

"Get lost!"

She felt bad for saying it the moment he was gone.

Too many things were lost already.

True swaggered like a winner, but lost his homework on a regular basis. He lost his wallet, his keys. He lost three films he'd checked out from the library and the fine was accumulating rapidly. This caused him to pull his whole bed out from the wall and look under it, so he found seventeen things he had been looking for, but not the films. He lost his own toothbrush, which made everyone in the family laugh at him. "How could you lose a toothbrush? Did you take it to school?" He tried organizational helpmates—a stacking-baskets desk device, a cheaper version of a PalmPilot. But he couldn't keep track of his own systems.

True simply didn't find organization interesting. To carry one's pants straight to the laundry hamper upon removing them was not what one *felt* like doing after a long day. You felt like throwing them on the floor with your keys in the pocket.

But Florrie thought disorganization caused people to lose time later, so she took great care moment by moment to be deliberate—sweater folded back into the drawer—dirty clothes pitched where they belonged. Her mother said it was a girl-boy thing, but Della was even more of a slob than True, so that was hard to believe.

Get lost. Bad words. Florrie should never have said them.

The following morning before school, True returned to the doorway of Florrie's room. She rarely hounded him from the doorway of his own, since it involved *climbing the stairs*. She had risen at five and had just finished grappling with geometric equations, feeling as if the top of her head had been carved into triangles.

"What are you doing?" he asked.

"Overthrowing the government. What does it

look like? How *do* you finish your homework so fast?"

"Study hall. I told you wrong. There are at least three Wal-Marts in Vermont. I looked it up on the Internet."

"Sweet of you."

"But the citizens of Rutland made the store move into their downtown, so it would bring traffic downtown. They made it use an already existing building."

"Great. I guess that's better than nothing."

"Aren't you happy?"

"No. I would be happy if superstores didn't exist." Now she turned her face to look at him. "But hey, thanks! You cared enough to look it up!"

True shimmied his hands in the air and swiveled his hips. "I just hate—you know—inaccuracies," which made her laugh out loud. He was incredibly handsome—for a brother.

14 ⁓ el viento

"I TRUST THE WIND"
BY FLORRIE HAMZA-ROMO

Hani Hamza moved to San Antonio from his village home in Lebanon when he was a teenager in 1933. "A big wind blew me from one side of the ocean to the other," he used to say. As a child he loved to cook with his mother and aunts, very rare for a boy of that period, and he dreamed of travel—so one could say my grandfather fulfilled his destiny.

When he started his restaurant in 1943 with Rita Lopez, the Mexican-American girl he married, he named it El Viento, "wind" in Spanish. He had great admiration for wind. He would step out onto the sidewalk whenever a chilly norther blew in, to feel it lift his hair.

His restaurant kept the same location for all the years of his life, in a downtown brick building next door to Solo Serve, one of the first help-yourself variety stores in the country. Solo Serve (founded in 1919) sold bolts of bright fabrics and racks of fancy dresses at discount prices. Women lined up outside Solo Serve on sale days. Hani said it was "a mob scene." They often spilled over into El Viento after shopping, hungry for tacos and tortilla soup, so he always had plenty of customers.

*Hani welcomed people with old-country courtesy. "Madame, I have your table just waiting for you!" Although he spoke Arabic, French, and English when he came to the United States, he tried to spice his conversations with Spanish words that he learned. His daughter Della (my mother) remembers how sometimes he would mix languages and irritate his wife (her mother). "*Bueno, yallah! *Yeah, yeah,* merci.*"*

Hani used to say, "El Viento belongs to nobody," which seemed mysterious to us when we were children, but made Rita mad. Did that mean he wasn't responsible if their restaurant was a failure?

His son-in-law Ruben Romo (my father) says, "What I loved first about Della's dad were his philosophical, nonchalant pronouncements."

I remember Hani saying things like, "I trust the wind," or "The wind sends me customers." My Grandma Rita used to say, "He should have been a weatherman."

Della remembers her mother whispering to customers while counting out change. "You think this place is my idea? I wanted to be a dress designer!" Rita drew fashion models wearing fancy jackets with big shoulders on the napkins.

At first Hani kept a few Arabic dishes—tabbooleh salad, stuffed grape leaves, baba ghanouj—mingled in among the chalupas and quesadillas on the menu, but they seemed to confuse people, so he took them out.

Mr. Tony Tiffin, our grandfather's best friend who used to eat at El Viento every night for years, says the restaurant has always had a "cozy" quality, which is what made him want to come there so often in the begining.

Della began working in the restaurant alongside her parents when she was a teen and in fact met my father, a young newspaper reporter then covering the police beat, there. She waited on his table. He smiled at her when she refilled his iced tea and said, "You are kind." For just refilling a glass.

Della mentioned him to her mother later. "Did you see the tall guy with the wavy black hair eating alone?"

"I saw him," Rita said, folding kitchen towels. "He looked sad."

The next time Della saw Ruben, he asked her out on a date.

So one could say the wind was in charge of her life, too.

Rita died a few years after my brother and I were

born. We do not really remember her very well. Our mother became the second-in-command at the restaurant then, working alongside her dad.

My brother and I loved our Grandpa Hani for many reasons. He always seemed calm. He always had time for us, even when cartons of tomatoes were being delivered through the back door and flats of Coca-Cola were being heaved into place. Hani would wave his hand at the delivery men, "You know what to do!" and turn back to us. He wore khaki pants, flannel shirts, and his smooth face was fragrant with aftershave.

In fact, he was the one person in our lives besides our neighbor Ingrid (also his friend) who always had time for us.

Parents tend to be preoccupied.

Hani let us stack pennies on his desk. I drew funny faces on his calendar and he didn't mind. He let us play with wads of tortilla dough. True always took his dough home in his pocket, where it would turn up in the dryer, a hard, pale lump.

He taught us simple Arabic words. "Say la *for* 'NO'! LA-LA-LA! *And people will think you are singing!"*

Hani carried a giant ring of keys in his pocket, with a miniature yellow harmonica and silver mila-gro charms (an eye and a foot) attached to the loop. He let us play with his keys and never said, "Be care-ful." He let us throw the keys on the floor to hear the clang. Sometimes the waitresses tripped on them. Our mother called it "that dangerous key chain."

Hani treasured odd details about San Antonio, his adopted city. He loved curiosities, strange names in the telephone directory, and the rare historic coins framed in the basement of Frost Bank. He liked the Alamo Music Center's sign, MUSIC MAKES KIDS SMARTER. *He liked the Shrine of the Little Flower, the Miracle Chapel, and Comanche Hill. Maybe he should have been a tour guide.*

Hani also loved the Mercado in the old days when it was a real farmer's market selling fresh fruits and vegetables. It reminded him of the ancient souks in

Lebanon. He bought us papayas and paper-thin goat-milk patties from Mexico. But he did not like what had happened to the Mercado in his last years, how it had turned into a crowd of stalls selling trinkets. He would close his eyes and say, "I'm looking at what used to be here."

On the city map, his favorite streets were Can't Stop, Eager, and Riddle. Knowing little things was a way he could belong.

His favorite question to us was, "What do you love?"

I always answered, "The same things that you love."

True always answered, "You."

Some evenings, when we were at the restaurant waiting for our mother to get off work, Hani would say to her, "We're taking an air break," and reach for our hands. We would step outside into the softening light. Black grackles swirled high above our heads, shouting and roosting in the trees. I was scared of them. Solo Serve was in its last few years. Soon it would close down forever and sit vacant. But the sign would stay there. It is still there now.

We would walk down Soledad to Dolorosa, over around San Fernando and City Hall, or take a turn up Houston Street, past the Majestic Theater and the waiting limousines. Buses and trolleys jingled and clanged and roared. It was a very nice break from the restaurant.

"Look at that," Hani would say to us, pointing at the carved gargoyles on the Tower Life Building or the swirls and swiggles on the facade of the abandoned Aztec Theater. "Isn't that something?"

Hani also loved stones—he lined the front window of El Viento with large white "friendship rocks," which he picked up on occasional hikes and drives around the hill country on Sundays. My brother and I sometimes went with him, to towns like Bandera or Vanderpool, driving slowly with the windows rolled down, leaning out, waving our arms, to feel the breeze. He never told us not to do that like our parents did.

We used to worry that someone might steal a stone.

Hani said, "So what? I stole them already, from the ground. Take it with my blessing. Maybe someone else will put another one down later to take its place."

Sure enough, kids and their parents started adding stones from summer trips to the windowsill. The ledge became crammed with shiny crystal geodes, cracked black beach stones, smooth whites from Maine, Big Bend desert rocks with delicate pink filigree. Customers looked for their own stones when they returned to the restaurant to eat.

Twice a year our mother Della collected the rocks in her apron, washed them, dusted the windowsill, and arranged them back in a line again. She still does that. She says it is like "a job a nitwit would be assigned to do in a penitentiary." She enjoys it.

Hani died suddenly in his sleep when my brother and I were ten and eleven. Things were very hard after that, because he was such a popular person. Our mother kept bursting into tears when customers asked for him or expressed sympathy. She wished for a farewell message, like a note. She even ransacked the *cash drawer. But she never found one.*

My brother, True, and our father never have been able to talk about him much.

I, on the other hand, feel his presence still permeating the green Formica tables and metal chairs and cracked red booths. His whistle still lives in the walls and the clatter of the plastic trays. My mother says sometimes she looks at something in the kitchen—the knob on the big oven, the refrigerator handle—and thinks, my daddy touched that. I do that, too. I remember his attitude, which retained great optimism even when Lebanon had its civil war.

Hani Hamza in his new country was a self-made success. Recently the manager at the Saint Anthony Hotel told me I am just as strange as he was, and I took that as the greatest compliment I will ever have.

His restaurant is still packed with customers and now we do catering. The catering boxes say, "EL VIENTO—SPEED OF WIND."

15 ~ a piece of fresh fruit

Tuesday morning at 7:30 A.M., Florrie was sitting outside in a green iron chair at the patio table, stirring hard knots of brown sugar into a very large bowl of clumpy Irish oatmeal when True came out the back door.

"You won't believe what happened this morning at five A.M.," Florrie said to him.

"I'm sure I won't, since I have never been up at that hour in my entire life," said True glumly, spreading peanut butter and jalapeno jelly between two slices of sourdough toast.

Since they were little, they had liked eating breakfast on the brick patio under the ancient pecan tree. It made them feel as if they were on a picnic holiday, except in summer, when webworms spun their disgusting gauzy nests. "So why don't you just tell me?"

He was always grumpy in the mornings. Florrie had read that splashing cold water on one's wrists was the best way to come to Full Alert Attention upon rising, but True was not interested in her tip.

"Well, I was sitting right here on the patio reading William Faulkner," said Florrie, "when I heard something knocking hard inside that silver bucket and realized the bucket was upside down. Something was under it, banging to get out. It scared me to death! I knew it wasn't Napper, because I'd just fed him on the deck, so what was it? A squirrel? A frog? The bucket was bumping loudly and moving around!"

She paused a long time and chewed. True glared at her.

"Do I have to invite you to go on with your story

or is this simply a pause for effect? *What was under the bucket?* God, that's enough oatmeal to feed the whole senior class."

"Well, I was scared to look. I mean, it could have run at me. Charged me like a bull or something. If it was a rat, wouldn't that have been nasty? So I came in and got the broom. I thought about getting you. I stood on a patio chair and tipped the bucket up with the end of the broom . . ."

"And? And?"

"It was a dove! A huge, fat, gray dove! It flew away as fast as it could. It was more scared than I was. But tell me this—how would a dove get under a bucket?"

True stared at her, shook his head, and slipped the sports section out of the newspaper. Their father never worked on the sports section so it was more relaxing to read. You didn't have to worry about misprints or stupid headlines.

"I guess it sat on the edge of the bucket and the bucket tipped over on it," Florrie mused, thinking,

Probably I should have saved the story for Lizzie instead of wasting it on True.

"Hmm—feel free to entertain your thoughts all by yourself now. I respect privacy. Or why don't you do a *science project*?" He took a violent bite of his toast.

"Well, I thought it was kind of—amazing— that's all." Florrie smiled, took the front section of the newspaper, and carefully smoothed it out in front of her.

Energetic finches with bright red breasts chattered and fluttered above them on the bird feeder. "Tim Duncan took another fall. Watch that knee, man," True said.

Florrie mumbled, "Tim is great."

Then she turned back to the front page, leaned her eyes very close to the page as if she were losing her eyesight, and burst into tears.

True said nothing. They could hear the recycling truck clattering down the street. Then he sighed. "Okay, now what?"

"After ninety-seven years! I can't believe it!" she shouted. "They're auctioning it off!" She paused as she read, her left hand frozen in the air. Tears were shining on her cheeks.

"The Kerr Mercantile General Store in Sanderson, Texas—don't you remember it? That big old-fashioned store where we used to stop on our way to Big Bend? You and Dad bought cinnamon rolls and I bought those purple bandannas and gave them to everyone for Christmas? *Remember?* We bought juice from that big red cooler box? The counters—the cash registers—they auctioned everything off this weekend! This says the store is no more! It was Sanderson's only store!"

True didn't say a word, but she kept talking. "Listen to this! Someone says, 'Right now, you can't buy a piece of fresh fruit in Sanderson.' The town judge says, 'It's the end of an era . . . devastating. Big old tears are running down my cheeks.'"

True sighed. "Well, it's too bad you weren't out there with them, then. You would have fit right in." He snatched the section out of her hand. "Maybe you shouldn't be allowed to read the newspaper. And why am I always the only one here to listen to you?"

But she kept talking. "It's an epidemic! What's wrong with everyone? Why didn't they fight to hang on to their treasure?"

"Florrie, it was a *store*. It wasn't a box of gold." True scanned the article and poked at it. "And read further—Mr. Kerr was probably a tired guy, okay? Look, Florrie, look here, his wife says he worked eighteen hours a day seven days a week."

"But why didn't more people *help him*? If the townspeople knew they were in danger of losing their only store, why didn't they buy more stuff? Why didn't they form a cooperative to keep it open? Why didn't they figure it out so they didn't have to *lose it*?" Her face was flushed deep red.

"Write them a letter. Tell them you loved their

store. And let's finish our breakfast in peace, okay? Because I have a truly stressful day waiting for me and Sanderson, Texas, is, like, three hundred miles from here."

"No," Florrie said. "I mean yes. I'll write a letter. But I'll do more too. Otherwise we are *doomed*."

Her spoon clanged angrily against the side of her bowl.

True stared at her. "You know, you might want to start getting psychiatric help very soon. Remember, depression can be genetic; it's not your *fault*. . . ."

"I am not depressed, I am *outraged*. There is a difference! You'll see! Nobody is talking about what big losers we are! We have GOT TO WAKE UP!"

"Believe me, I am now awake."

Their father stepped out the back door pointing at his watch. Florrie ran past him into the house with her empty bowl and the tears still glistening on her cheeks.

"What's going on?" Ruben asked True. "Tell me you two weren't arguing so early in the morning."

True sighed. "Dad, it *is* possible your daughter is loony tunes. As her most frequent witness, I can testify. Other families have normal problems—divorce, alcoholism, drugs, bulimia. But we have Grandma Moses with a punk haircut worrying about things that don't even belong to her."

16 ~ floating campaign

Not everything worked out.

The rally for the Aztec Theater was a big bust. Only Bailey, wearing a Palestinian *keffiyah* around his neck, and creaky Tiffin, wagging a bedraggled cheerleader pom-pom from Operation Friendship, appeared with signs, BRING BACK THE AZTEC!!!!! People waiting at the bus stop sniffed at their minor display and made no comment. Florrie thought they should have planned it better. Maybe they should have dressed as Aztec gods.

* * *

Florrie's own mother stopped at a Target to buy some detergent, and also bought a new, classy teapot while she was there. When Florrie saw the empty plastic bag on the kitchen counter, she confronted her mother, who swore she had momentarily forgotten about the boycott. "I just drove into the parking lot automatically, thinking about all the laundry piling up."

"How could you?" demanded Florrie.

"Baby, you have no idea how many things are in my mind."

At Thanksgiving Florrie tried to get her mother to give her the entire front window again for a giant poster to customers: WE ARE THANKFUL FOR ALL OF YOU, but her mother still declined. A small poster was all she would allow. "I don't want people to get mad at me," Della said.

Florrie said, "*What* people? What are you talking about?"

"Like people whose husbands or wives work for

corporations or franchises. If they think I hold myself above them, they might stop eating here."

"Mom, that's ridiculous! Fear of what other people think will cause you not to speak up?"

"I guess so, baby. I guess so."

Florrie did receive some fan mail—from the manager at Schilo's Delicatessen, who appreciated "her efforts on behalf of all of us." She pinned it to her bare bedroom wall.

Lizzie said, "I think we have made a good public statement, don't you? I'm feeling ready for the boycott to be over because I really want some of those soft fleece jackets and vests that people are getting at Old Navy. I hate my old lumpy sweaters. Those fleece things are only ten dollars! Besides, what about all the Christmas presents we'll need to buy?"

Florrie said, "Odd little shops are the best places for Christmas presents, silly!"

* * *

There were only two weeks left in the official boycott and Florrie worried that things were going to end on a weak note. Although she knew she would never enter a franchise again in her entire life if she could help it, she couldn't ask that of everyone. She wished she could. She had told them "till the end of the year" and said that beyond that time, they could all be advocates in whatever ways they chose. But she wanted to end the official campaign with a flourish.

When she had called a special meeting at the schoolyard's cement picnic tables to discuss the closing of the Kerr Mercantile General Store in Sanderson, wondering if they could take a trip out to far west Texas during the Christmas holidays and try to kick up a little dust of action, Bailey shook his head and Lizzie sniffed. "It's too far," she said.

Bailey said, "We don't know anyone there."

Florrie said, "So we *meet* them! It takes approximately five minutes to start knowing someone. We give them a little boost of care and inspiration. We tell them we don't want Sanderson to die!"

But nobody jumped at her idea.

Who had a canoe? Florrie knew Mike Casey, a friendly lawyer in her neighborhood who wore a dapper bowtie and rode his one-speed bicycle with a basket all over downtown. He often pedaled to El Viento, chaining his bike to a pipe in the alley while he ate. He kept a flock of chickens and a giant turkey named Elena in his backyard. Sometimes he gave Florrie's family fresh eggs. And he had a canoe.

Ruben had interviewed him once for a story on people who lived, by choice, without air-conditioning—a rare breed in hot southern climes.

If Mike Casey had a canoe, wouldn't he know other people who had canoes? This was the way the world worked. You didn't have to know everything, you just had to know who to *ask*.

Florrie figured about four canoes and eight paddles would do the trick. Did they need life jackets?

The San Antonio River was so narrow that if anyone fell out they could easily be rescued, even if they couldn't swim. Anyhow, they'd have a champion swimmer with them.

Official boating permits were obtainable from the River Authority for free, if you wanted to canoe along the botanical bend of the river, away from the waterside cafés and bars and music clubs. But that was not what Florrie wanted.

She and Zip, Ramsey and Juan and Bailey, Lizzie and Beth, were going to launch the canoes upstream, by the Southwest School of Art & Craft, at the peak of the Saturday dinner hour, 7 P.M. They would drift slowly downstream, paddling when they needed to, and appear in front of the diners drinking salty margaritas alongside the riverbank. They would wave their giant signs.

SUPPORT INDEPENDENT BUSINESSES!

BOYCOTT FRANCHISES!

KEEP SAN ANTONIO SCENIC!

SAY NO TO CHAINS!

They would make friends and enemies at the same time. Paesano's Riverwalk, a great Italian restaurant run by an old local family, would like them. Boudro's would like them. So would Casa Rio, an old-time Mexican restaurant sporting cheery umbrella tables.

The Hard Rock Café would not like them. The Hyatt Regency by the water would not. But who cared what they liked? They were not Originals. Mike Casey promised to be eating Boudro's crab cakes at a table by the water to see them go by. He would cheer for them. He would eavesdrop on what other diners said.

Florrie felt terribly pepped up about it all but, since she was the organizer, tried to act calm. First Juan had to pick up the canoes and get them to the proper launching point upriver. He was driving his battered station wagon around for two hours on Saturday afternoon, following maps Florrie gave him, with a different canoe tied onto the roof each trip.

He deposited the canoes and paddles at a secret place behind some dense hedges near the art school. He left Zip to guard them, next to some graffiti on the wall that said, "If life is a bore, don't horde, dance more, stop war." They all agreed that this was pretty good for graffiti.

Zip brought *The Tempest*, their new English assignment, and read it sprawled behind the bushes. "I should have been down here doing my homework for *years*," he said later. Though it was December, and cool, the temperature had been hitting sixty-five to seventy during the days, so the air felt perfect.

Zip had suggested they all wear hats. He was always thinking of photo opportunities, how they might look on the evening news. Florrie thought hats made her look like a turtle, but she complied. She wore a navy blue baseball hat borrowed from True that said "Big Bend." Zip wore a red Pharaohs Country Club hat from Corpus Christi with a stitched picture of an Egyptian pharaoh on it.

She wished more people would show up other than her trusty few friends who had promised to come. Were they getting sick of her? Did she only imagine people had started avoiding her at school? But if more people came, there wouldn't be enough boats for them. They could walk alongside the river and cheer or something.

Beth came skipping down the River Walk, a flashlight in her right hand. "Just in case!" she said, grinning, holding it up. She wore a handmade baggy orange sweater and a crocheted beret made of rainbow yarn. She had taken the bus.

Lizzie, Bailey, and Juan showed up five minutes before launch time. Lizzie was wearing her tattered blue-jean jacket with the Virgin of Guadalupe on the back, in sequins. Bailey wore a giant tuxedo jacket from the Salvation Army and a Spurs hat. He said, "I figured this would be my main party of the holiday season." Where was Ramsey? "Look out!" Lizzie (cowboy hat with spangled hat band) shouted at Juan (black Mi Tierra cap backward) as he tipped a canoe too far to the right and she almost toppled into the water. "I don't want to ride around all wet!" Bailey started laughing.

"Take it easy, Lizzo," Juan said. "Zip and Bailey are riding with you. They're smooth guys. They won't dunk you."

"YO!"

It was Ramsey's voice echoing out from under the bridge, as he walked toward them with a girl. They were tipping their heads back, sharing a laugh. When they got closer, he raised one arm. "The tribe thickens!"

Florrie tried to swallow the sudden blockage in her throat. She attempted to smile and greet them, but found herself coughing instead. Ramsey had not mentioned bringing anyone else. She noticed they wore no hats. She had left him a message about hats the day before and had not heard back from him.

"Amanda," he said, sweeping his hand in front of the girl in a group introduction and kissing Florrie

on the cheek. Amanda grinned and wagged a tiny hand.

"Hi guys!" Ramsey said to all the others. "You look ready for action! What a crew!" Florrie's friends nodded, mumbled, tipped their hats.

Ramsey wobbled the green canoe back and forth, as if he were testing something. Amanda reached out and placed her hand on his back to balance him. Florrie felt befuddled. Was she staring at them with her mouth wide open? She quickly tried to busy herself, leaning over the silver canoe and pushing it forward, but Juan said, "Wait! We'll help you."

Ramsey tossed two paddles into the green canoe after setting it afloat. He stepped into the boat first, reaching his hand out to help Amanda stay steady—she carried a sign and a glittery purse. *A purse? Why does she need a purse?*

Who was she? And why did her jaw have that attractive straight slant?

Of course Florrie had planned to ride with

Ramsey, but now she was stuck with Juan. She craned her neck to read Amanda's sign. KEEP SAN ANTONIO DISTINCTIVE, it said. That, at least, was good. That was one of the slogans they had all decided on, so Ramsey *had* received some of the messages. Florrie had sent him a list of suggested sign slogans by e-mail.

Zip, Lizzie, and Bailey were already floating. Lizzie held two signs since she was the passenger in the middle. They were speaking low in the boat, saying things Florrie couldn't hear. "Don't forget!" she called to everyone. "If we see a tourist barge or any of those barges crammed with Christmas carolers, we have to paddle over to the side immediately, as fast as we can."

"Right!" called Bailey. "You know, this is like the first Christmas activity I have participated in on the river since I was a shepherd in the posada— was anyone else a shepherd?"

"I was Joseph," said Juan.

Florrie felt embarrassed as they all pushed off

from the riverbank on their mission. She should be thinking, *Menger Hotel, we're doing this for you! Viva El Viento and the Mexican Manhattan!*

But she was having superficial thoughts.

She was thinking: *He* brought *her.* Her hair so sleek and deep brown and long. *Should I have cut my hair?* Her breasts under a snug blue long-sleeved T-shirt and her perfect, tight, low-cut jeans. When she stepped into their canoe, a large swath of bare skin was visible above the back of her jeans. Florrie noticed both Zip and Juan staring from behind. Probably checking to see if she had a tattoo. Ramsey, Ramsey. Why had he never mentioned Amanda?

They paddled south past the giant cypress trees that had stood for a century, guardians of the quiet water. Some had intricate root systems at sidewalk level. Florrie used to sit inside the giant roots when she was little and dream of the fairies and elves living in the mossy compartments, and the squirrels cooking supper in the dark.

They paddled past an elderly Mexican-American couple sitting on a bench arm in arm. Couples like that gave Florrie a strange whiff of nostalgia. When was the last time she had seen her parents arm in arm?

The river meandered between the buildings, curved to the left, and split in two. Soon their canoes would reach the busy district. All the trees were strung with thousands of looping colored lights for Christmas. It looked incredible. Florrie called out, "Can you believe it? Once this river was almost *paved over*! And now it's the city's big tourist attraction."

"How can you pave over a river?" Zip shouted.

It was strange to call out from canoe to canoe.

"Well, I guess you could make it like a drainage ditch," said Juan. "Just build over it and stuff. Hide it."

"Women saved it!" shouted Florrie. "Activist women!"

"Really?" said Lizzie. "Are there fish in here?"

Juan was peering over the edge of the boat into

the dark water. "Of course there are fish. There are always fish. Look, minnows! But are there snakes? Are there turtles?"

"Sure," said Florrie. "*Lots* of turtles! All sizes. Probably my own old turtle among them. South of my house, people come down to the river with buckets and fishing poles and stuff. Cane poles. You can see the turtles swimming if you look down from the Alamo Street Bridge by Blue Star. Some are *huge*!"

It was amazing to Florrie that Lizzie had lived in San Antonio all her life, and hung out at Florrie's house, and still didn't know things like this.

Bailey said, "I think it would be nasty to eat a fish out of this river."

"It's nasty to eat fish, period! And shrimp are the scavengers of the sea!" shouted Zip.

Florrie had an odd thought—sometimes it was more fun to think about things in advance than to actually do them. She had been secretly plotting this river escapade for weeks. But now that their paddles were dipping into the shallow green water, canoes drifting right and left of a central beeline, she could feel the wistful edge of concentration.

Amanda tossed her hair back and beamed. "I *hate* seafood!" she called out joyously. (Did anyone care?) "But I am so *so* hungry for a nacho!" Florrie noticed Zip, Juan, and Bailey smiling vaguely, as if they wished they could provide one. Lizzie chimed, "God, I'm starving, too!"

Now they were gliding into the commercial district, neon-gilded cafés and noisy music bars materializing up ahead. They passed La Mansión del Rio, the white hotel with balconies where Lyle Lovett liked to stay. "There's Sky!" Zip shouted, pointing up. "Turn your signs toward his camera." Everyone waved and pumped their fists in the air for Sky.

Zip had asked his friend Sky, a video student at San Antonio College, to stand on the bridge next to La Mansión and film them. Zip thought their canoe protest could be included in Sky's project on "voices of the city." As they drifted under the bridge, Zip introduced Sky to Ramsey and Amanda, pointing and calling out. They turned their canoes around, lumbering to coordinate their paddling, and floated back under the bridge to make sure Sky got good footage of all the signs. This caused many people on the banks to turn and look at them.

Ramsey called to Zip, "You three-letter-name guys have great ideas."

Amanda giggled and said, "Byeeeeee, Sky!" as they paddled on.

They passed old buildings renovated as apartments—new begonia pots and cozy lamps in high-up windowsills.

"You know, Florrie, this is *your* neighborhood," Zip called out, "so don't you think your canoe should go first?" Ramsey was back-paddling. "Be our guest," he said, waving Florrie ahead. Amanda's perfect laugh slid out between her luminous teeth.

Grrrrrrrrrrrrrrrr. Florrie and Juan floated past them toward front and center.

The canoes passed under a graceful footbridge. Was Dick's Last Resort a franchise? Strains of music snagged in the trees—riffs of jazz from The Landing, sweet accordion twists of *conjunto* from some little bar. Tourists leaned on one another, spellbound by reflected lights, staring at all the places they might stop to drink or eat, then turning their heads (a few of them) to the river. Florrie wondered how easy their signs were to read in the dusk. At least the walkways were well lit. Should they call out their sign's messages to attract more attention? Was that disturbing the peace?

Florrie tried it out, calling, "KEEP SAN ANTONIO DISTINCTIVE!" A few heads turned. "Please!" Then she said, "Thank you!"

"Hi!" shouted Beth sweetly, to an older couple who were staring at her. "Hello, diners! Please eat in independent restaurants!"

"I think we're crashing!" Juan shouted. He back-paddled madly away from a cypress trunk curving down to the water. Florrie tipped left, dropped her sign onto the damp floor of the canoe, and began paddling harder herself.

"Viva Paesano's!" she shouted, seeing the restaurant's neon sign. She picked hers up again. The maitre d' standing by the sidewalk with menus tucked under his arm waved at her. Her parents went there for anniversaries to eat their famous creamy garlic shrimp. Florrie could see Zip's canoe drifting over at the other bank and some kids beside the river calling out to Zip's crew. Did they want a ride? They passed Justin's Italian Ice and Florrie called out, in case he was inside working, "Justin! Hey Justin!"

Unexpectedly Florrie laughed out loud. *You could dream things and see them happen.* Even if they didn't feel quite the way you imagined they would, the night would be dark, loops of blue and yellow lights reflecting in the water, small waves lapping against the sides of the canoes, your voices held high, on sticks. You could stand up for things, or sit down for them, or float . . . and this was a happiness worth living for . . . Suddenly a sharp spotlight shone onto Florrie's face. Someone was standing on the bridge above them shining it.

"STOP RIGHT THERE!" A loud voice spoke through a megaphone. Their boat was drifting backward. It was hard to control. "I said, 'STOP!'"

Well, there wasn't a brake in a canoe. "It's not that easy!" she called out. *Who is that?*

"Bring your boats to the side of the river and hold them right there. Don't move, any of you."

"Is it a police officer?" Juan sounded worried.

"Peace, gentlemen!" Ramsey called out. "This is a peaceful demonstration."

Florrie spoke to Juan in a low and worried voice as they paddled mightily toward the bank. "Texas waters are public places. I checked." It occurred to her now, however, that no one ever saw a personal canoe or rowboat scooting among the tourist barges on the river. Canoes were only allowed, with permits, farther downstream. No doubt the restaurants and night clubs had purchased some kind of usage right for the commercial stretch of the river that kept private individuals from actualizing their boating fantasies. She should have thought of this before.

As Florrie blinked in the high-voltage beam, she could see three young policemen awaiting them at the bank. They had stepped down from the bridge to the river's edge. One was crouching. Another had his hands on his hips. He called out, "Do you mind telling us what you're doing?"

Florrie noticed the dull handle of a shiny revolver clamped in the holster at his waist. She felt herself gazing at it.

These were the sturdy bicycle policemen who wore blue shorts and patroled downtown. Florrie had seen them pull over cars before and felt impressed that someone on a bicycle could pull over a car.

"Protesting!" Ramsey shouted with gusto.

"Excuse me?"

"Rallying!" Florrie said. "Reminding people! To eat and shop at the independent places we have left. We love San Antonio! Save San Antonio!"

There was one good moment when all four canoes were clustered together, held to the bank by the staunch oars, and the policemen actually looked at the signs. Then they looked at one another.

A very nice-faced one said, "You wanna cause a barge wreck? You think it would be okay if every Tom, Dick, and whoever threw a boat into the river whenever they felt like it and rode around? Funny, huh?"

"Not funny. Serious!" shouted Florrie.

Amanda giggled.

"Well, we urge you to pull those boats out of the river right here and now. Seriously. Move it!"

Amanda leaped gracefully onto the bank, balancing her own paddle and sign. Florrie felt her heart zooming and thudding inside her chest, hitting the walls. Beth looked very nervous. Florrie and the other girls scrambled out onto land.

Then Bailey and Juan and Ramsey and Zip heaved the boats onto the bank, which was not easy to do. Florrie scrambled to collect the paddles and signs. Sky, who had been trailing them along the River Walk, was now filming the policemen. One turned to him and said, "CUT! Turn that thing off."

"Okay, we're not going to charge you with anything, since—at the moment—there's a little dispute going on about the river, like who has jurisdiction over which part of it . . . but we *are* going to tell you not to do this again, ever, got it?"

"Could we walk up and down the river with our signs?"

"Do you have a parade permit? I don't think so."

Florrie gulped. "Could we just stand in a spot and speak to everyone who passes? And hold our signs? That's not a parade."

One of the policemen turned to study Florrie. "Girl, are you relentless or what?"

"She *is*," Ramsey interjected. "Relentless." Though it might have felt like a compliment at another time, or coming from someone else, it hurt her feelings at that moment.

Dragging the boats up the steep stairs to the street level was difficult.

Lizzie and Beth, unbelievably, had a sudden need for ice cream cones and headed down the block to a little ice cream stand by Rio Rio. The boys went to get the cars, leaving Amanda and Florrie to stand with the canoes at the corner of Commerce and Navarro.

Florrie said, "Oh no, Mike Casey!" She snapped her fingers.

Amanda said, "Who's that?"

"He's our friend who loaned us a canoe. He was waiting to see us pass by and is probably wondering what happened to us."

"This was sort of cool," Amanda said, swinging her glittery purse in one hand, doing a little street-side twirl. Florrie felt like socking her.

A fire engine screamed past. A car pulled over to them and paused a moment, as if someone were going to get out, then screeched its tires pulling away. A stretch limo passed looking ridiculous.

Florrie swallowed hard, but made herself ask it. "Have you and Ramsey—been friends long?"

"Oh, forever. You know, Alamo Heights. We went to elementary and junior high school together . . . but our friendship has sort of—changed—recently." Amanda smiled, one hand on her hip as if she had a twist in her back.

What did she mean by that?

Amanda continued, "We're going to go over and get something to eat at the Liberty after this—you want to come?"

Florrie had introduced Ramsey to the Liberty Bar over on Josephine Street. She had gone there since she was little, with Grandpa Hani especially. He loved the crooked white wooden restaurant (it used to be a pool hall) that sat tipped on its weathered moorings and looked as if it might fall over in a strong wind. It served "serious food"—beet salads with oranges, corn chowder, and a fat portobello mushroom sandwich on homemade bread. Ramsey had eaten the whole plate of free bread slathered with butter. He had kissed Florrie's hand there, held it tightly with both his own hands, and told her the Liberty was "their place."

"I don't think so," Florrie said to Amanda, feeling a weird twist of emotion toward her, as if grateful for the attempted inclusion. "I'm not eating tonight. I mean, this got all messed up. Plus, we have to take these canoes back. . . ."

A grandmother with a giant pocketbook over her shoulder and three tiny kids in tow passed them speaking in Spanish. A horse clomped by with a bride and groom still dressed in wedding clothes seated majestically in a white carriage, looking stupefied and radiant. Fake flower bouquets were clipped to the sides of the carriage atop huge pink satin bows. "Congratulations!"

Amanda chirped to them, waving. They waved back shyly.

Finally Zip's station wagon pulled into the no-parking zone, followed by Juan's. They turned on their flashers. Lizzie and Beth walked up with their giant double-dip chocolate cones. "Too bad," said Lizzie. "It was just starting to feel really fun when it ended. Hey Florrie, did you want ice cream? We should have asked you. Want a lick?" Florrie shook her head no. Ramsey pulled up a moment later. The boys heaved two canoes onto Zip's roof, coupling them together, and stuck the other two into the open back end of Juan's station wagon. Zip, who somehow knew how to tie solid knots, raced around with the ropes. Juan checked his watch and said he was going to a free outdoor concert at the Sunken Gardens. Did anyone want to come? Lizzie said she did.

"I'm sorry this event wasn't more successful!" Florrie said, to nobody and everybody. "Thanks for everything! The signs were really good. Keep them! I'll think of a new plan."

"Good try, mate," Ramsey said to Florrie, patting her shoulder.

What, was he suddenly Australian?

He did not mention the Liberty Bar. Amanda turned to hug Florrie before hopping into his car. She pressed her large breasts tightly against Florrie's own more modest chest. "He is *really* amused by your antics," she said confidentially, as if Florrie were a hamster. "And I wanted to see some for myself. Ciao!"

17 ～ hot wells

Florrie leaned against the front car door gloomily, pressing her chin into her fist, as she and Zip drove the canoes home. "How did you learn to tie such good knots?" she asked him.

"Boy Scouts, baby. We learned how to build good fires, too. You need any fires?"

They took one canoe back down to the Hot Wells neighborhood on the south side. Zip drove very slowly, with the Trinity jazz station playing softly.

"What should we have done differently?" Florrie mused out loud. "Maybe we should have gotten a powerful businessman to sponsor us. So they couldn't just throw us out like that. Maybe a restaurant. Or a city councilperson. Someone besides ourselves. No, that's what everyone does. I would hate to be sponsored by somebody else. It would make us like a commercial."

Zip glanced at her. He was used to her talking to herself.

"Or maybe we should just have gotten that parade permit and walked along with our signs. Then we could have talked to people easily. Maybe the canoes were irrelevant. Too dramatic."

"So, we try again. What's stopping us?" he asked.

"Oh, I don't know. Nobody really cares."

They dropped the last canoe over an iron fence into the owner's yard (a historic house called "The Castle") then drove back north toward downtown on South Presa Street. South Presa was lined with junky bars, car parts shops, tiny cottage motels from the fifties, and blue stucco pool halls.

"Any place you want to stop?" Zip asked her hopefully. She had often made him drive her down to the place in the road across from the railroad tracks where they could see the towering ruins of the old abandoned Hot Wells spa. The ruins, looking like a burned-out castle for real, loomed over a dense stretch of pecan trees.

Ingrid had at least a hundred Hot Wells postcards from the spa's heyday when a direct trolley line connected it to downtown. Back then fancy people, movie stars and politicians, came from all over the country to dip into the hot healing mineral waters. Little round metal tables sat under the trees for gracious outdoor dining.

Someday Hot Wells would come to life again. The capped springs would be unleashed and the sulphurous healing water would bubble forth again to fill the old-fashioned pools. "Diving Prohibited" said the giant painted sign on the crumbling brick wall. The lettering was still strong, after years of abandonment. Florrie and Zip had once sneaked into the grounds at sundown to look for Teddy Roosevelt's signature over a doorway.

But tonight she was silent in her seat, slumped low. "No thanks. But thanks."

"You're not really too sad, are you? The river demonstration was a great idea, Florrie! And it *was* fun while it lasted. Maybe it made an impression on *somebody*."

"Besides us and the policemen, you mean? Take me home, please," she said.

"You wanna go bowling at Hermann Sons? Or is this bingo night? You wanna play bingo?"

"Home."

Zip sighed. "I'm afraid you aren't much fun anymore, old friend. Work, work, work. Old Zip may have to find a new girlfriend."

"I am *not* your girlfriend. I have not been your girlfriend *in many years*."

His face fell. He looked straight ahead and drove without speaking.

Then she felt sorry for him. She pinned her eyes on the blue stripes of neon, the highway overpass, cars whizzing toward Houston. People could feel like ruins, too. She wished she were far, far away.

They drove a few miles in silence. A long train was crossing Probandt, the railroad crossing-arm down. Zip turned the car off, knowing how Florrie hated to idle. She said it made her sick to her stomach.

"Well," he said, sighing. "I did have one nice update to tell you. Wanna hear it or not? I spread our campaign to Houston last week. When I went to that science fair event. And it was the major topic at the lunch table. Not science! People were really interested."

Florrie managed a slow grin. "Really?"

He said, "I told them about you and how you got us all going. I also spread the idea to Stafford and Shiner, because two of my good science fair buds live in Stafford and my cousin lives in Shiner. He said his mother has been missing the Palace Café for years! And all these junky things are coming in and the town is losing its flavor . . . so they said they would be happy to get some folks together and do just what we've been doing. And you know what? It would be even easier to make an impact in a small town, don't you think? Like, spreading the word and the boycott, getting people involved . . ."

He broke off. Florrie was staring at him with a glazed expression.

"Stafford?" she said. "Stafford, Texas?"

"Of course! It's a cool town. Near Brenham, where they make the ice cream."

"I know. I've been there. A long time ago. With my dad, when we drove home from Mobile . . ."

"When did you go to Mobile?"

So she sat there and she told him, the same story she had recently told Ramsey. She told him about the cheesy grits in thick white bowls and the two ladies, one black, one white, in white aprons, ladling up the food, and the old calendar on the wall, and the way her dad had said, "Look closely, soon you won't see places like this. . . ."

Zip did not say anything cute or interrupt her.

He just listened. He took her hand and pressed it to his lips, then his forehead, as if he were inventing a new ritual. He said, "I don't have to be your boyfriend if you will always, always just talk to me."

The train had stopped. They sat in silence, comfortably. Finally it backed up a few cars and rolled forward out of the way.

She kissed him very softly and slowly, on the lips, when she got out of the car. He seemed a little shocked. "I think we're comrades for life," Florrie said. "We will probably end up living together when we are very very old."

18 ~ froth

The river parade did not make the newspapers. A reporter would hardly have had time to come down to the riverbank. It would live on in their memories alone.

But someone named Mrs. Groos, a famous San Antonio name, had written a letter to the editor touting their project in general and saying that anyone who hadn't participated should be *horsewhipped*. "Just drive out toward Taft High School, along franchise row, and you'll know how crucial it is that we hang on to what we have. The franchise boom along I-10 is an insult to our creativity! We must follow the fine example our youngsters are setting."

Florrie called Lizzie. "Are we youngsters?"

Lizzie said, "Oh yeah, that's my neighbor. She's really getting into this."

As Florrie was unlocking the front door after school a few days later, she could hear the telephone ringing and ringing. But the caller was hanging up just as she touched it.

Sometimes you could stare at a telephone and hypnotize it into ringing again. Florrie's dad would not spring for Caller ID or call waiting or any modern telephone device. He would not let them use *69 because *it cost money.* When the phone rang in the evenings, it was usually some guy selling plots at the cemetery—did anyone really buy those by telephone? *Oh great, I feel the flu coming on, why don't I just go ahead and take two?*

Zip called on his usual regular basis. Had she heard anything about the rumor that Bob Dylan might perform in the Sunken Gardens soon?

Could she please tell him again exactly what was that horrible assignment they had to do on *Much Ado About Nothing?* He irritated her by asking how the "guy with the sheep's name was." As if someone called Zip had any room to talk.

But Ramsey had not phoned since the night at the river. One week you were kissing somebody and the next . . . it was like when a war ended. Everyone just acted normal again. Cooking and eating and complaining about regular things like the price of grapes or the weather. *Unless they had lost a loved one,* she thought. *Then they were changed forever.*

Should she call Ramsey? He had Caller ID. She dialed twice, then hung up before the ringing started. Maybe something bad had happened to him. Friends should check up on one another when someone just—disappeared. This wasn't 1950. In 1950 girls waited for boys to call.

Or maybe Amanda had taken off her shirt. Ramsey had asked Florrie if she wanted to take off her shirt one day when they sat by the river behind the big bushes south of the St. Peter-St. Joseph Children's Home and she had said no. Not really. Not here. Not today.

One Saturday about two weeks after the river parade, Florrie impulsively dialed and Ramsey's mother answered. What a proper, cheery voice she had.

"Is Ramsey there please?" Florrie's own voice sounded squeaky.

"He is not. May I take a message?"

"No, umm. I'll catch him later."

"Is this Florrie?"

"Umm—yes. I just hoped he wasn't sick or anything."

"He's not sick at all; he's fine. He's just out with some friends. I'll tell him you called."

Would she really?

When Florrie hung up, she felt even worse. Now if he didn't call, she would know his silence was intentional.

Out with his friends? Well, of course. Ramsey had lived a long time before meeting her. He had a million friends. Probably they didn't get arrested in their recreational time. Probably they went to movies and Starbucks.

Starbucks! What time was it? Four-thirty. The perfect Starbucks hour. Hadn't he told her he often went there before he met her to drink chai? Hadn't she tried to get him to give it up?

She dialed the Starbucks nearest his house. She couldn't believe she was doing this. Even as she dialed, a little voice in her head said, *You are pathetic. What do you need? You need to know he misses you? You think you'll like him less if you find him at a franchise?*

The cappucino machine was frothing at the mouth right next to the phone receiver.

"Sorry to bother you, but could you see if you have a customer there named Ramsey, please?"

She waited a long, long time. People were ordering sweet coffee drinks with ice. She could hear the sound of milk hissing into a cup. Probably they had forgotten about her.

Finally someone picked up the phone and said, "May I help you?" It was a different voice. "Are you holding for someone?"

"For Ramsey," Florrie said.

"Oh. He doesn't seem to be here. Sorry!" The phone banged down.

An hour later Ramsey called.

"Hey!" he said. "My mom said you rang. How's it going?"

"Well!" She gulped. *Stay calm. Don't act too excited.* "I was worried about you."

"Worried?" He laughed. "Why?"

"Haven't two weeks or so passed? You've been very quiet."

"Sorry, a lot's been going on." He sounded matter-of-fact. He didn't seem very sorry at all. There was a loud sound, as if he'd dropped the phone, then he spoke again, more softly. "Are you okay?"

She tried to sound breezy. "Have you been avoiding me on purpose? That's what I figured!"

"Why would I do that? No! I should have called. I mean, I tried a few times. . . . You know I told you my parents are . . . They get into their moods . . . I told them about the canoes since it was all so funny, you know, and they didn't really respond. . . ."

"So that's what!" said Florrie. "They hate me."

"What do you mean? Of course they don't hate you. How could they? They don't know you! But they did think, umm, maybe I should, you know, we're asking for trouble. . . . They think . . ."

"I'm a bad influence."

"Sort of."

She didn't know what to say to this. There were ways one could not defend oneself. He said, "Hey, I've missed you."

"You have not." But she was glad he said it.

She regretted later that she told him, "I even called Starbucks looking for you." *That was pathetic.*

"I was there! A minute ago! Takeout!" He laughed nervously. "I should have gone to Espuma. Ouch!"

"No. Yes. "

"But it's in your neighborhood, not mine. Too far out of my way."

Then he said, "Could I come by and see you tomorrow?"

"Sure! When?"

"Well—" He paused. "Depends on when I'll be able to get away. I think my parents said we are going to brunch at the Saint Anthony. My cousins are in town. Could I come after that? I'll call to make sure you're home."

"Of course," she said, later thinking, *I should have said, Maybe.*

The next day came and he did not call. Hours passed; the rain poured down. She listened to Keb' Mo' and Pete Yorn; she composed a few rough drafts of letters to editors. She read a magazine—celebrities complaining how hard it was to have people staring at them everywhere they went (*They should be refugees,* she thought)—and an old *Utne Reader,* which Ruben had left on the couch.

When she entered True's room to talk to him, she thought, *I must be desperate.* True was instant messaging nine people at once, his screen a patchwork quilt of chatter. He said without turning his head, "*What?*"

"You didn't like Ramsey much, did you?"

"Nope. Not much. Why?"

"I think we won't be seeing each other anymore."

"Good."

Now he turned his head. "Are you okay? He was a jerk."

"No," said Florrie. "He was not a jerk. Maybe he wasn't who I hoped he was. But he was not a jerk."

"I got you a present."

"Why?"

He nodded at a sack lying on his bed. She

dumped out a soft cotton yellow shirt with rounded white buttons. He said, "From that vintage store over on South Alamo. I stopped in to check on the suit of armor they had in the window. We were thinking of using it for our Spanish project if it was cheap enough but it wasn't. He said we could rent it, maybe. Anyway. I saw that shirt. Feel how soft it is. Can you help me with *Wuthering Heights*?"

"But it's yellow."

He turned and smiled at her. "Yellow looks great with gray. You're going to branch out to yellow any minute now. I can feel it."

At 10:30 P.M. Florrie went out front to the porch and stared into the pearly light around the street lamps. Maybe she would let her hair grow out, too. Tie it up in a little pig's tail on top. Her father had gone to bed early, her mother was still at the restaurant, and True was now watching a disgusting movie about cars that drove very fast.

Florrie began swinging back and forth on the

porch swing like she used to when she was a little girl. She dangled her legs. *Well, the hell with him.* She should just have said, "Amanda?" and he could have said, "Amanda!" and they would have been more honest. *Forget his hair and the smell of his neck. Forget, forget, forget.*

After she got a little dizzy, she walked around back and stared into the river, soft yellow circles of light reflected from the walkway lamps. She could see the dark clumps of sleeping ducks by the riverbank.

How could it be that someone with whom you spent so many delicious hours could just—disappear? Replace you?

She took a deep breath.

As if you were an old abandoned building in a—city?

She smiled when she thought that.

At least she wasn't alone.

She ran back into the house, up the spiral staircase, and plopped down on True's bed beside him.

He looked shocked. "Could we watch something else?" she asked.

"*We?*" he said.

He put out his hand to fend her off. "You want something. Get away from me. You must want something."

19 ~ next door

At 11 P.M., True drove six blocks over to pick up their mother. Della strode into the house saying, "I can't believe it." She pitched her purse onto the fat blue-and-white checkered chair across from the television. "I absolutely can't believe it. The nerve!"

"What's wrong?" Florrie was curled on the couch, wearing her green pajamas with old-fashioned calendar pages printed on them (that she had bought at Banana Republic before she stopped shopping there), eating a bowl of crunchy granola, attempting to read her history assignment.

How could she love history so much and hate

the official history that was taught at the very same time? Official history revolved around battles. Power. Who seized it, who lost it. Politics. Manipulation and men. Too many men. *Her* history revolved around German acrobats doing handstands on long-vanished Bowen's Island in the San Antonio River and great blue herons standing on one leg in the river just behind her house.

"You won't believe who's moving in next door!"

"Next door?" Florrie sat bolt upright. Ingrid had gone to live with her niece across town while her fractured hip mended, but she came to visit every weekend and pointed her cane at everything in her yard that needed to be swept and trimmed.

"No, not here—at the restaurant! In part of the old Solo Serve space!" Della was speaking at a loud volume.

Their father swung open the door of the bedroom and stepped into the living room, bleary eyed, looking irritated. "Why are you talking so loudly? You *know* I can't go back to sleep when I get waked up." He plopped gloomily down onto the same chair with Della's purse, sitting on it.

"Oh! Sorry," Della said. "Did you hear? Who's coming? "

"King Kong?" asked True.

"Taco Bell."

"No."

Florrie's mouth opened wide. Taco Hell next to El Viento? Were they crazy?

"That's *disgusting*! Well, don't worry about it, Mom! No one will eat there."

"You say not? So why are Taco Bells sprouting up like mushrooms all over the country?"

"Don't worry! No one eats there except boys in pants sagging down off their hips and desperate parents with screaming children. You won't miss them much."

"That is not true. Many *many* people eat there."

"But your customers won't. They love you."

Della went into the kitchen and banged some

pots around. Was it possible she was really going to cook? At this hour? All three of them followed her. Ruben pulled the pitcher of ice water from the refrigerator and started pouring himself a tall glass. Florrie said, "Dad, I want some." She was holding onto both sides of the doorway, swinging herself back and forth like she used to do when she was a little girl. Ruben reached for a second glass. True unfolded a bag of popcorn and popped it into the microwave, whistling.

Ruben began emptying the dishwasher as Della sliced some jalapeno peppers. "Mom," Florrie said softly, "you want me to do a rally for you?"

Silence. "What do you mean?"

"We could have a Restaurant Appreciation Day for El Viento! Serve everything, say, at original prices, like Hani used to charge, you know, cheap! Weren't there twenty-cent bean tacos or something? We could copy that first menu framed on the wall. Maybe hire a few mariachis, display big signs urging people to support their trusty independent restaurants and not be satisfied with tasteless taco items from cardboard factories. You wouldn't have to name any names . . . so they couldn't, like, sue us or anything. What do you say?"

There was a silence. Florrie noticed the dark circles under her mother's eyes. Then Della asked, "Don't you think it's obvious, though? That our food's better than their food?"

"Of course it is! But an appreciation rally would get attention! Make people think! Remind them of what they should never forget! We could make a press release, invite journalists and my TV station friends, too!"

Now Della was frying onions. Unbelievable. She had plopped two tomatoes into a pan of boiling water.

"Mom, what on earth are you doing?"

"I thought a couple of *huevos rancheros* might comfort me. You want some? I brought a few corn tortillas in my purse. . . ."

"No way, it's the middle of the night!"

True was sitting in the window seat in the kitchen, stuffing his hand into the steaming popcorn bag and grinning. "It's a family moment!" he said.

Florrie pulled up the old white metal stool. Her grandfather had kept it in the corner of his own kitchen when she was small. She used to sit on it, legs dangling, while he pressed grapefruit halves onto his spinning electric juicer. The stool had a dented place on one side.

She crossed her legs and watched her mother.

Ruben was leaning against the counter now. "I'll have some with you," he said to Della. He was always hungry when he woke up.

Florrie was talking as she thought. "Hmm—we could invite the mayor to speak? We've never thought of that before!"

"Oh honey, you've thought of enough," Della said. But she was smiling. She was looking happier. "Maybe you—*we*—could get someone very old to describe the chili vendors who used to surround Courthouse Square—hmm. Because they were all little businesspeople of the most extreme variety. You know, as a kind of historical record. Could Ingrid do it?"

Florrie said, "Why not? She talks as good as ever! She's just slow on steps."

Della ruminated out loud. "I was thinking of those chili stands recently . . . you know, from the pictures on your postcards. . . . I pass by where they used to be twice a day. . . . How nice it would be if they still existed. Red-checkered tablecloths. Giant pots, big spoons . . . I wouldn't mind *their* competition."

Florrie was musing hard. "You know, Ingrid would be great. *That* would be a catchy little news item! Her birthday is coming up. '100-Year-Old Makes Public Plea.' God, I'm starting to think like Dad! I'll call her tomorrow."

Ruben said, "Is it such a bad thing to think like Dad?"

Florrie continued. "Maybe the guy from Eddie's Tailor Shop would speak—he is very eloquent on this subject. We could serve chalupas? Three kinds of enchiladas. My friends could help us wait on everybody!"

Della was nodding hard. True was crunching popcorn. Ruben was digging in the drawer for what was left of a rolled-up bag of tortilla chips. "Sounds like the front page again to me!" he said. "At least of the metro section."

Florrie continued, "My friends love free food. We'll have fanfare. We'll go crazy."

"You think?" Della cracked the eggs into the skillet. They sizzled. The sauce bubbled up around them. "Should we do it? Will anyone notice?"

Florrie hugged her tightly from behind. "Well, will anyone notice if we just stay quiet till every little thing we love is gone?"

acknowledgments

For Florrie McCard and True McManus, wishing you beautiful lives and hoping there will still be real buildings and eccentric enterprises in the world when you grow up. (Hope you won't mind that I borrowed your great first names! Same goes for Della Hobrecht and Reuben Nye, in memory.)

Thanks to Frank Jennings for his ongoing love and care for history and urban environments.

In honor of Patricia Lucille Osmond Osborne and her landmark work on behalf of historic preservation in San Antonio. "Thank God you could look at an old building and see the sacredness of the people who walked there. Thank God you saw more than new malls and greed wherever you looked."—Fr. Bill Davis, at Pat's memorial service.

Also in honor of Maury Maverick, Jr., Herschel Bernard, Julia Cauthorn, Dan Anthony, Bernard Lifshutz, and Ilse Griffith.